TELLING SECRETS

"Hey, relax," Carole joked nervously. "Just because a movie star is in love with your girlfriend, that doesn't mean every guy in the world wants to steal her away from you."

Alex stopped short. Slowly he turned to face Carole again, his face pale. "What did you just say?"

Carole giggled nervously, feeling more uncomfortable than ever. Maybe that hadn't been the most tactful joke in the world—Alex was probably still sensitive about the whole topic. But once again, her mouth seemed to have become detached from her brain as she hastened to explain herself. "N-Never mind," she stammered. "Um, I just meant, you know, the thing with Skye—how he told Lisa over the summer that he liked her as more than a friend . . . You know."

"No." Alex's voice had gone as cold as ice. He turned away from Carole to stare grimly at Lisa. "As a matter of fact, I didn't know. Thanks for letting me in on the secret."

**Don't miss any of the excitement
at PINE HOLLOW,
where friends come first:**

PINE HOLLOW™

PENALTY POINTS

BY BONNIE BRYANT

BANTAM BOOKS
NEW YORK • TORONTO • LONDON • SYDNEY • AUCKLAND

Special thanks to Sir "B" Farms and Laura and Vinny Marino

RL 5.0, age 12 and up

PENALTY POINTS

A Bantam Book / August 1999

"Pine Hollow" is a trademark of Bonnie Bryant Hiller.

ISBN 0-553-49285-3

Published simultaneously in the United States and Canada.

Bantam Books are published by Bantam Books, a division of Random
House, Inc. Its trademark, consisting of the words "Bantam Books" and
the portrayal of a rooster, is Registered in U.S. Patent and Trademark
Office and in other countries. Marca Registrada. Bantam Books, 1540
Broadway, New York, New York 10036.

PRINTED IN THE UNITED STATES OF AMERICA

OPM   0 9 8 7 6 5 4 3 2 1

My special thanks to Catherine Hapka for her help in the writing of this book.

ONE

"Hey there," Lisa Atwood said softly as she opened the stall door and slipped inside. "How's my favorite mommy-to-be?"

The resident of the stall, a long-legged Thoroughbred mare, snorted and took a step toward her. Lisa smiled as the horse snuffled at her jeans pockets and then moved her big, velvety nose up and down the front of her shirt.

"Sorry, Prancer. No treats today." Lisa reached up to smooth back her hair as the horse ran her nose over it experimentally, obviously still hoping to discover a stray carrot or slice of apple. "Just wanted to come for a little visit with you and the babies."

She shook her head slightly as she said it, automatically running her eyes over the mare's glossy bay flanks. Prancer was almost three months pregnant, but a stranger would have had trouble spotting the slight swelling of her belly.

1

Even Lisa, who had ridden Prancer for years, had trouble seeing it.

She also had a little trouble believing it. Lisa had fallen in love with Prancer, a former racehorse, when the mare had first come to Pine Hollow Stables years before. Since then she had rarely ridden another horse—at least until a few months earlier, when she had left her home in Willow Creek, Virginia, to spend the summer with her father in California. When she'd returned just before the start of her senior year, everything had changed. Prancer had been bred with the Pine hollow stallion, Geronimo, and was pregnant—with twins, no less. The mare couldn't be ridden until her foals were weaned, by which time Lisa would have departed for college.

Lisa had been trying to reconcile herself to that fact when she had found out that her father was planning a surprise for her: He wanted to buy Prancer for her once the foaling process was finished. That news had been almost as unsettling as the news about the pregnancy itself. Knowing that the sweet, willing, beautiful Thoroughbred would someday be hers had made it both easier and harder for Lisa to deal with the mare's pregnancy. Easier because she knew that her days of riding Prancer wouldn't be over, even if she went far away to college the next year. Harder because it made her worry more than ever about all the things that could go wrong in the coming months, especially since Prancer was carrying twins, which was very rare and risky in horses. In her seventeen years, Lisa had rarely felt as many conflicting emotions about anything—happiness, terror, anticipation, and worry tumbled through her every time she thought about the tiny foals growing inside Prancer.

"It doesn't seem to bother you one bit, though, does it, girl?" Lisa murmured, gazing at the mare's calm, wise, gentle face. Without thinking, she stretched her arms around Prancer's neck and stood on tiptoes to plant a kiss squarely on the horse's smooth, soft cheek.

At that moment she heard a shuffling sound nearby. Looking up quickly, she saw Carole Hanson standing in the aisle outside, peering at her over the half door of the stall. Lisa had met Carole and her other best friend, Stevie Lake, when she'd started riding at Pine Hollow four years earlier. Since then the three girls had been virtually inseparable, spending countless hours together talking, riding, and sharing their common love of horses. Back when they had first met, they had even formed their own club, The Saddle Club, as an excuse to spend even more time thinking and talking about their favorite subject. Now that they were all in high school, there never seemed to be enough time for the hours-long gab sessions and endless sleepovers of their middle-school days. But despite all the new distractions and pressures of their lives, they remained close.

"Can't a girl and her horse have a little privacy around here?" Lisa joked weakly, feeling her face turn red as she loosened her embrace. She felt slightly foolish that someone had caught her kissing a horse like an overenthusiastic new rider. Still, she knew that Carole would understand if anyone would. Carole loved horses so much that she had taken on a part-time job at Pine Hollow, turning her hobby into the beginning of what she planned to be her lifelong career. Max Regnery, the owner of Pine Hollow, often commented that Carole thought more like a horse than the horses themselves.

"Sorry. Didn't mean to interrupt." Carole smiled, but she seemed distracted.

Lisa noticed that her friend's expressive, deep brown eyes held an anxious look. "Hey, are you okay? Is something wrong?"

"I hope not." Carole tugged distractedly on the end of her shoulder-length black braid as she

4

stared at Prancer. "But we won't know for sure until Judy comes back."

"Judy?" Lisa felt a quick stab of worry, realizing that her friend was referring to Judy Barker, the veterinarian who treated the horses at Pine Hollow. "What do you mean? Is something wrong with Prancer?"

"Well, Max isn't sure, but he hasn't been able to detect the second foal's heartbeat for the last day or so, and—"

Lisa gasped. "What?" Her heart started to beat faster and fear washed over her as she glanced at Prancer. "Are you sure? I mean, is he sure? I mean—"

"Hold it." Carole reached over the half door and took Lisa's arm. "Let me finish, okay? We don't know anything for sure right now. There's no sense in panicking."

Easy for you to say, Lisa thought quickly. *She's not your horse.*

But she didn't say it aloud, knowing immediately that she wasn't being fair. Carole cared so much about horses—*all* horses—that if something were wrong with Prancer or either of her unborn foals, Carole would feel it as deeply as Lisa would.

Taking a deep breath, Lisa did her best to stay calm. "Okay," she said, gripping the edge of the stall door for support. "Now tell me. What exactly do you know?"

"Practically nothing," Carole admitted, lifting her hand to stroke Prancer's neck as the mare stretched her head over the door to say hello. "It's just as I told you. Max can only find one heartbeat, which could mean nothing. Or . . ."

She didn't finish the sentence, but Lisa shuddered. Ever since she'd found out that Prancer was carrying twins, she had learned more than she'd ever wanted to know about the risks of such pregnancies in horses. She knew that it was rare for a mare to carry both foals to term, and that a lot of things could go wrong in the eleven long months of gestation. She knew the odds, but she still maintained her hope that Prancer and her babies would beat those odds and come through all right in the end.

"So where's Judy, then?" she asked, doing her best to quell the tide of panic that kept rising inside her. She put a hand on Prancer's warm, smooth neck, trying to calm herself with the mare's large, solid, living presence. "Why isn't she here right now checking on her?"

"She was on her way, but she got called off to another stable for a case of severe colic. She said she'll try to stop by tonight if she can, but we probably shouldn't hold our breath." Carole shot

Lisa a sympathetic look. "Seriously, though. I know it's kind of scary, especially after all we've been hearing about everything that could happen. But Prancer obviously isn't in any distress"—she waved a hand to indicate the mare, who had turned away from the girls to snuffle at her hayrack—"so we probably shouldn't worry yet—not until we know there's something to worry about."

Lisa shuffled her feet in the deep layer of straw covering the stall floor, trying to take Carole's advice. But she knew herself. She knew that she'd go crazy if she stayed there with Prancer, worrying and wondering. The only way to retain even a few shreds of her sanity was to distract herself somehow. "You're right," she said, thinking aloud. "And I know the best way to keep our minds off this. What do you say to a nice long trail ride? Just you and me."

Glancing at her watch, Carole shook her head slowly. "Sorry," she said. "I don't think I'd better. I told Max I'd help him with some paperwork before I left today, and I want to allow plenty of time to work on Samson's gait changes, and then I—"

"Oh, come on." Lisa tried not to sound as desperate as she felt. She needed help to have any hope of taking her mind off this new, unsettling news. If she had to sit around alone with nothing to do but think about it, she wouldn't be able to stop imagining all the terrible things that could happen. Her mother was working, her boyfriend, Alex, was at soccer practice, and Stevie had a student government meeting that would probably last until dinnertime. That meant that Carole was her best hope for company. "Come on, please? I'm sure Max wouldn't mind if you took a little break. I mean, how long has it been since we just went on a nice, long, relaxing ride in the woods? You've been training so hard for that horse show with Samson, poor Starlight's probably forgotten what you look like by now."

Carole checked her watch again. Then she looked at Prancer and finally turned her gaze to Lisa. She still looked reluctant, but she nodded. "Well, all right," she agreed. "Maybe I can make time for a quick ride. And you're right, Starlight could use some exercise. So who do you want to ride?"

"Who do you suggest?" Even though Prancer's condition had kept her out of circulation for more than eight weeks now, it still felt strange for Lisa to have to consider which horse to take out on the trail.

Carole pondered the question for a moment, and Lisa could tell she was running through her mental list of Pine Hollow's horses. Lisa leaned on the half door and waited patiently, glad that she'd managed to talk Carole into the ride. *It will probably be just as good for her as it'll be for me,* she thought. *Carole works awfully hard at her job here, and lately, with preparations for that horse show eating up even more of her time, she's been positively crazed.*

Max had recently invited Carole, Stevie, and several other riders to represent Pine Hollow at a prestigious horse show being held in the neighboring town of Colesford in a few weeks. Carole was to ride one of Max's horses, Samson, in the show. Samson was talented, but he was also young and relatively inexperienced, at least compared to the other horses that would be competing in the Colesford show. Carole had been working like a fiend to get in as much training as possible before the show, which meant that she hadn't had much time for anything else—including fun. Lisa was a big believer in the value of hard work—her steady stream of A's in school were proof of that—but she also knew that it sometimes paid to take a break.

"Well, there weren't any group lessons today," Carole said thoughtfully. "So you can pretty much take your pick. How about Eve? You got along well with her the last time you rode her."

"Sounds good." Lisa nodded. Eve was an eager, gentle, silvery gray mare who was a favorite of many Pine Hollow riders. With one last pat for Prancer, Lisa reached for the stall door. "I'll go tack her up. Meet you at the horseshoe in ten minutes."

Exactly ten minutes later Carole was in Starlight's saddle, stretching her hand toward the good-luck horseshoe on the wall. The smooth old horseshoe had been nailed to the wall since long before any of the current riders could remember. Nobody even knew who had started the tradition that every rider should touch it before heading out, trusting in its power to keep them safe from accidents on the trail. After brushing the worn metal of the horseshoe with her fingers, Carole patted her horse and wondered how many times the two of them had stood there together, ready to enter the schooling ring for a riding lesson or to explore the miles of trails in the forests and fields that stretched off behind Pine Hollow.

"Ready to go?" she asked Lisa.

Lisa was bent over in Eve's saddle, adjusting her left stirrup. "In a sec."

Hearing steady hoofbeats from somewhere nearby, Carole glanced outside. She nudged Starlight forward a few steps until she came within view of the main schooling ring, where a lone rider was cantering in a tight circle.

Carole sat still in Starlight's saddle and watched with admiration as Ben Marlow guided a spirited young dapple gray mare surely around and around, asking her to change leads on each rotation. The horse, Firefly, was new to the stable, and Max had asked Carole and Ben, one of his stable hands, to take over her training. With a pang of guilt, Carole realized that she couldn't remember the last time she'd worked with the feisty gray. *I guess it's a good thing Ben's been holding up his end of the bargain,* she thought ruefully. *He's lucky—he doesn't have to deal with school on top of everything we have to do here.*

She shifted her gaze from the mare to her rider. Ben had graduated from high school the year before, and he'd been working full-time at Pine Hollow ever since. Carole had recently discovered that, like her, Ben harbored hopes of someday receiving a college degree in equine studies. In his case, however, that goal seemed all but hopeless. He didn't have the money to pay for school, and a recent attempt at obtaining a scholarship to a local program had failed.

Carole hadn't talked much with Ben about any of it, though. He was an intensely private

11

person, and even though Carole sometimes suspected she was as close a friend as he'd ever had, she still couldn't quite bring herself to brave his brusque and sensitive temper to pry further into his thoughts and feelings, which all seemed to hide somewhere just behind his dark, brooding eyes.

"Okay." Lisa's voice broke into Carole's thoughts, and she started.

"Huh?" she said. "Oh, um, okay. Ready." She gathered up her reins and clucked to Starlight briskly, not wanting Lisa to notice how she'd been staring at Ben. She suspected that even her best friends didn't really understand her interest in the young stable hand. Like most people, they'd been turned off long before by his silent ways and sullen attitude. But Carole couldn't give up on him that easily. She'd seen his wonderful rapport with horses, who all responded to him as enthusiastically as people stayed away from him. To her, that alone made Ben worth knowing.

Carole did her best to forget about Ben as she and Lisa rode across the fields behind the stable at a leisurely trot. It was a cool, brilliant October day, and every blade of grass seemed to gleam under the clear light of the afternoon sun. The leaves in the forest beyond the fields were starting to show their autumn colors, and even the horses seemed to breathe deeper as they moved through the clean, crisp air.

Taking an extra-deep breath herself, Carole had to admit that she was glad she'd allowed Lisa to talk her into going for a ride. She'd only said yes because she had sensed that her friend really needed to relax after hearing the latest about Prancer. Some people were surprised to find that, beneath her mature, sensible, perfectionist exterior, Lisa could be quite emotional—especially concerning the people and horses she loved. Carole, however, wasn't surprised at all that even a hint of trouble with Prancer's pregnancy had set Lisa worrying. Some people might see Prancer as just another animal, but to Lisa she was practically a part of her family. Glancing at her friend's back just ahead of her, Carole was glad she'd been there to help distract her. She clucked to Starlight, simultaneously giving him the signal to lengthen his stride. Soon she was riding beside Lisa at a steady trot. "This is nice," she called to her.

Lisa nodded, glancing over and smiling. "Thanks again for coming with me. I know you have a lot to do to get ready for Colesford—"

"It's okay." Carole felt a brief thrill of anxiety at the thought of the show. She had hoped to spend at least an hour and a half with Samson that day, practicing some important basics like gait changes and turns to make sure they were ready for the intense competition of the show. She quickly shook off her worry, not wanting Lisa to notice it and feel bad. "You know what they say about all work and no fun. . . ."

Lisa brought Eve to a walk, and Carole did likewise with Starlight. "Actually, I think the saying is 'All work and no play,' " Lisa corrected with a smile. "But speaking of fun, have you talked to Stevie lately? I wonder how the party plans are going."

Carole realized that she'd almost forgotten about Saturday's big bash. Stevie was throwing a party at her house, with some help from her longtime boyfriend, Phil Marsten, and her twin brother, Alex, who also happened to be Lisa's boyfriend. It was going to be a good-bye party for another friend, Emily Williams, who was moving to Australia with her family the following week. Stevie didn't take many things seriously, but planning a party was an exception. Carole was sure that with her friend in charge, Saturday night would be an evening to remember.

"I haven't spoken to her in a couple of days," Carole told Lisa as the girls walked their horses side by side toward the woods. "But last I heard, she'd invited practically all of Willow Creek. She's been promising everyone it will be the party of the century."

"Sounds like a true Stevie Lake production," Lisa said with a laugh. "Emily will love it." She sighed. "I just hope we're not still worrying about Prancer by then so we can enjoy ourselves."

"Don't worry," Carole reassured her. "It's only Wednesday, remember? I'm sure Judy will stop by tomorrow, if not sooner, and she'll be able to tell us what's going on."

"I certainly hope so." Lisa pulled Eve's head up as the mare paused to sniff at a patch of wildflowers. "I don't think I can take much more suspense at this point."

Carole felt a flash of guilt, guessing that Lisa was remembering how she'd worried and wondered for weeks why Max wasn't letting anyone ride Prancer. By the time he had finally admitted to her that the horse was pregnant with twins, Lisa had practically worried herself into a frenzy, imagining that her beloved mare had every fatal ailment known to man or beast. Carole had known the truth all along, but she hadn't said anything to Lisa—she'd promised Max to keep the pregnancy a secret, and she took her prom-

15

ises seriously. When Lisa had discovered that Carole could have saved her all that anxiety, she had been furious with her. The two had made up since, but it was still a bit of a sore subject for both of them.

"It's weird," Lisa went on thoughtfully. "Doesn't it seem like nothing ever really gets finished anymore?"

"What do you mean?"

Lisa shifted her weight slightly in the saddle. "You know. Just when you think some crisis or whatever is over—or just when you think you know what's going on, or how to handle some problem—something else comes up. It never really ends, you know? You can never just wrap up all your problems and coast."

Carole glanced at her friend out of the corner of her eye, wondering why Lisa suddenly sounded so philosophical. *It must be Prancer,* she told herself. *She's got eight more months to go, and that really does seem like forever sometimes. Especially at times like this when we're afraid there might be a problem.*

"I know. But this pregnancy really won't last forever," Carole pointed out, steering Starlight around a rock outcropping in the field. "By the time Prancer's foals are weaned and you're riding her again, we'll probably wonder what we were all so worried about." They had almost reached the edge of the forest by now, and both horses were pricking their ears forward at the trees, as they always did.

"It's not just the pregnancy. It's more like everything. Things just seemed so much simpler before I went away, you know?" Lisa shrugged.

"Sure," Carole said uncertainly. "I guess." She wondered if Lisa was thinking about her mother, who had recently started dating a much younger man she'd met at work. Carole's mother had died several years before, and Carole knew firsthand that having a single parent who went out on dates could be pretty weird, especially when you didn't approve of the person they chose. She was about to say something to that effect when Lisa spoke up again, her words startling Carole out of her thoughts.

"Sometimes I wish I hadn't even gone to California at all."

"Really?" Carole was surprised. Even though she and Stevie had missed Lisa like crazy while she was gone and known that she'd missed them right back, she had thought that Lisa's West Coast experience had been mostly a positive one. She'd gotten to spend time with her father; her new stepmother, Evelyn; and her baby half sister, Lily. A bonus had been having the opportunity to see a lot of Skye Ransom, a popular young actor and an old friend of all three girls. Plus Skye had helped Lisa land an incredible job for the summer, working as a stable hand on the set of a new TV show set at a dude ranch. When she thought about it, Carole couldn't help thinking that that summer Lisa's life itself had sounded a little like some kind of glamorous TV show.

Lisa picked up on the surprise in Carole's voice and glanced over with a slight smile. "Okay, not really, I guess," she admitted. "I'm glad I went. But I can't help thinking sometimes that a lot of things would have been easier if I'd never gone."

"What do you mean?" Carole still felt perplexed. She sensed that they weren't only talking about Prancer anymore, or even Mrs. Atwood's new boyfriend, but she couldn't imagine what else was on Lisa's mind.

Lisa slowed Eve as they stepped into the cool shade of the forest edge. "Well, for one thing, obviously, I would have been riding Prancer all summer, so I probably would have known about it when Max decided to breed her." Her voice grew softer. "And, well, there wouldn't have been so many secrets."

For a second, Carole assumed again that she was talking about the secret that had come between them regarding Prancer's pregnancy. But something in Lisa's face—something faraway and almost wistful—made her think that might not be what she was referring to at all. "What secrets?"

Lisa hesitated. "Well . . ."

By now Carole was really curious. She wished Stevie were there—she wouldn't have had any qualms about dragging Lisa's thoughts out of her. "Um, you don't have to tell me, obviously," she said awkwardly. "But if you want to, you know you can trust me."

"You have to swear not to tell anyone." Lisa pulled Eve to a stop and turned to gaze at Carole seriously as Starlight drifted to a halt as well. "Not even Stevie."

Carole gulped, not liking the sound of that. But she nodded. "I promise. I won't breathe a word."

Lisa took a deep breath. "It's about Skye."

"Skye?"

"Right." Lisa bit her lower lip. "You see, something happened between us at the end of the summer—something I never told you and Stevie about. He said something . . . something about how he'd been thinking about what might have been—how things could have been different between us if—" She broke off, smiling

19

sheepishly. "Well, it doesn't sound like much when I put it that way. But basically he was letting me know that he wished there was a chance we could be more than just friends."

"Really? He said that?" Carole couldn't help feeling astonished. *How do these things happen?* she wondered, not for the first time. She had seen plenty of movies and TV shows and read lots of novels where people made similar pronouncements as a matter of course. Still, she had trouble imagining things like that happening in real life, to people she knew, in between the more everyday stuff like eating, doing homework, and mucking out stalls.

"He didn't put it in exactly those words, but it was pretty clear," Lisa confirmed. "He was as nice and understanding as could be about my relationship with Alex, and he told me he didn't want to ruin our friendship or anything, but he felt like he had to say something. Just so we would both know where we stood."

"Wow."

There was a moment of silence. Carole nudged Starlight with her foot, setting him walking again. Lisa did the same with Eve, and the two friends rode along, each lost in her own thoughts. Carole was still trying to figure out how these sorts of exciting, romantic things happened in real life, and why they never happened to her. *Not that I would know how to deal with it if a guy said something like that to me,* she thought ruefully. *I would probably totally misunderstand him and think he wanted to hire me to train his horse or something.*

"Anyway," Lisa went on after a moment, in a tone of voice that indicated she'd had enough of the discussion and was ready to end it, "as you can imagine, that little situation has caused some tension since I've been back. You know, with Alex."

Carole nodded, even though she couldn't really imagine it at all.

TWO

"**H**urry up with those balloons," Stevie ordered Phil briskly. "The party's tomorrow, you know, not next month."

Phil rolled his eyes and grabbed a handful of multicolored balloons out of the box next to him. "And Emily's sixteen, you know, not six," he joked. "Are you planning to hire a clown and set up some pony rides for this party, too?"

Stevie just snorted in response and leaned over from her seat on the living room sofa to check the clipboard at her feet, which held a list of things to do. She knew that balloons and streamers weren't exactly the decorations of choice at most high-school parties, but she didn't care. She wanted Emily to know that she was special enough to warrant a little extra effort. Besides, she figured the patriotic red-white-and-blue theme could only help with the other goal of this party. . . .

That thought brought her mind back to her favorite topic these days. "It's hard to believe Election Day is only a week and a half away," she commented, sitting up and running her hands through her long, thick, dark blond hair. "There's so much more to do before then. Still, Scott and I have really made some progress this week—he's such a natural campaigner that he makes my job look easy."

She smiled as she thought about the past week. Scott Forester was a senior at Fenton Hall, the private school that she and her brothers attended. Stevie had met him over the summer, soon after his family had moved to town from the West Coast to join his father, who had been elected to the U.S. House of Representatives the year before. Scott's sister, Callie, who was a junior like Stevie, had come to Pine Hollow because she was a competitive endurance rider—or at least she had been, before the car accident that had damaged her right leg and had temporarily paralyzed her whole right side. Callie was still learning to walk normally again, aided by three things: the metal crutches she used to get around, the therapeutic riding sessions she attended faithfully at Pine Hollow, and her own determined, proud, sometimes stubborn personality.

Scott could be just as determined as his sister, but he showed it in a much different way. Whereas Callie could sometimes come across to people who didn't know her well as aloof or haughty, Scott had a way of putting people at ease that made him instantly popular wherever he went. It was a quality he had inherited from his politician father, and it had made him a natural choice to fill the recently vacated post of student body president at Fenton Hall. Scott had asked Stevie to be his campaign manager, and she had thrown herself wholeheartedly into the job.

"I figure this party is a natural place for Scott to talk to a lot of people and get his ideas out there in a fun setting," Stevie mused, sitting back on the couch and rubbing her hands together excitedly. "Especially since Valerie Watkins will be out of town and can't steal any of his audience. Of the three people running against Scott, she's the only real contender."

"I know," Phil said patiently, tying off the balloon he'd blown up while Stevie was talking. "You mentioned that before. A few dozen times."

Stevie scratched her head thoughtfully, hardly hearing him. "Still, I think we have the edge. Valerie has been at Fenton Hall a lot longer than

Scott has, and she has some interesting ideas, but she's a little too quiet. Too shy about putting herself out there. I think when people hear what Scott has to say, they'll realize he's someone they can count on to get things done, you know?"

"Sure." Phil flicked the balloon across the room and reached for another. "You've already convinced me. But I can't vote, since I don't even go to Fenton Hall, remember?"

Again, Stevie hardly heard her boyfriend's comment. She was still thinking about Scott and his busy week of campaigning. "He's been trying to talk to everyone he can this week." She frowned slightly. "The only thing getting in his way is that he still won't tell Veronica to get lost. She keeps hanging around him all the time, flirting her head off and trying to distract him."

"Sounds like classic Veronica."

Stevie nodded sourly. Veronica diAngelo had never been one of her favorite people. *Why is it that nice people like Emily have to move away and obnoxious snobs like Veronica stay put?* she wondered. Veronica came from one of the wealthiest families in Willow Creek, and that had always given her the idea that she was better than everyone else. It had also given her the idea that she could have anything she wanted, and what she seemed to want at the moment was Scott Forester. Scott wasn't exactly giving her any encouragement in that direction, but he wasn't being *dis*couraging, either—at least not as far as Stevie could tell.

"I don't know how he puts up with her," Stevie muttered, kicking at a balloon that had drifted toward her. "I think that's the only downside of this past week's campaigning. I've had to spend *way* too much time with Veronica."

Phil grinned and reached over to poke her playfully in the side. "That's not the only downside. You were too busy making posters to meet me at the diner when I was hit by that sudden chocolate milk shake craving, remember?"

"It's a good thing," Stevie said pertly. "If you keep sucking down milk shakes the way you do, you're going to weigh nine hundred pounds by Thanksgiving."

Phil pretended to look insulted, but Stevie just grinned, running her eyes over his athletic, well-toned physique. She wondered idly, not for the first time, how she'd been lucky enough to find such a good-looking, wonderful boyfriend. *Of course, he's pretty lucky, too,* she reminded herself contentedly. *After all, he ended up with me!*

Soon, though, she found her mind drifting back to the election. "Anyway, I'm going to do my best to make sure that Scott spends some time talking to every Fenton Hall student who shows up tomorrow night," she said, tucking her legs up beneath her on the sofa and reaching into the box for a balloon. "I just hope Veronica doesn't get in the way too much." She grinned. "You'd knock her down and tie her up if I asked you to, right?"

"Hey, I didn't know this was going to be that kind of party," Phil said, pretending to look worried. "Neither did your folks, or they'd never have decided to leave town this weekend."

"Heh heh heh," Stevie cackled evilly. Then she grinned again. "Seriously, though, that reminds me—we owe Chad big-time. Despite all the brilliant arguments Alex and I came up with, I think the only reason Mom and Dad decided to leave us alone this weekend and still let us have the party was because they knew he'd be in town."

The day before, Mr. Lake had suddenly been called to New York City for an important business dinner on Saturday. Mrs. Lake had been tempted to go with him and make a weekend mini-vacation out of the trip, but when she had remembered Emily's party, she had thought better of it. Fortunately Stevie's oldest brother, Chad, a sophomore in college, had called at just the right moment to tell his parents that he was coming home to Willow Creek that weekend for an older friend's bachelor party. After he had promised to check on his younger siblings before and after his own party, and after Stevie and Alex had sworn that they would act no differently with their parents in another state than they would if they were sitting in their bedroom upstairs, Mr. and Mrs. Lake had reluctantly agreed to leave the kids alone for the weekend.

"When's Chad getting here?" Phil asked.

"Anytime now." Stevie glanced at her watch. Her parents had left an hour earlier, and so had her younger brother, Michael, who had made plans to spend the weekend at a friend's house along with the Lakes' dog. Alex was at Pine Hollow with Lisa, which meant that for the moment, Stevie and Phil had the house to themselves. "Which reminds me—we're wasting a golden opportunity here. Can you even remember the last time we were all alone in this house?"

"Heh heh heh," Phil replied, pushing the box of balloons off the sofa and scooting closer to her. "What exactly did you have in mind?" He draped one arm comfortably around her shoulders, put his other hand on her knee, and pulled her toward him.

Stevie's lips were just meeting his when she heard the front door slam.

"Yo! Anyone home?" Chad's voice rang out.

"Rats. Busted again," Stevie said, pushing Phil away. "Nothing kills a romantic mood like hearing your brother's voice, you know? Come on, let's go see if he remembered to pick up our soda when he got the supplies for his bachelor party."

She hurried into the hall with Phil at her heels. Chad was setting down a case of two-liter bottles of cola. Behind him, another guy was holding a shopping bag filled with chips, pretzels, and other snacks.

"Oh. Hi, Luke," Stevie said when she saw the second guy. "I didn't know you were coming."

Chad greeted Stevie and Phil cheerfully. "Luke needed a place to crash for the weekend, so I told him he could stay here," he explained. "Luke, you already know my sister. This is her boyfriend, Phil Marsten. Phil, this is my buddy Luke Chatham."

As the two guys shook hands, Stevie was careful to keep a pleasant smile on her face, not wanting Chad to guess her true feelings about his friend. She had only met Luke once or twice before, but she didn't like him much. She wasn't really sure why—usually Stevie liked just about everyone she met until they gave her a reason to

29

change her opinion. But something about Luke Chatham rubbed her the wrong way. She always had the sense that he was thinking something completely different from what he was saying and therefore couldn't quite be trusted.

"Come on, you two," Chad said when the introductions were over. "Luke's car doesn't lock, and we don't want to leave our stuff in there overnight. Help us carry it in."

Soon Stevie and Phil were standing by the trunk of Luke's battered old junker. Stevie wasn't surprised that the locks didn't work—she was much more surprised that the car had actually managed to make it the forty or so miles from the university without falling apart. "Nice ride," she said dryly.

Luke shot her a glance. "Hey, the radio works," he said. "What more do you need?" He cast a sidelong glance at Chad. "Except for a backseat, of course," he added with a playful leer. Walking to the back of the car, he opened the trunk. It was packed full of cans and bottles.

It wasn't until Stevie was holding one of the cases of cans that she realized it held six-packs of beer, not soda. "Whoa," she commented. "Hey, Chad, since when are you old enough to buy beer?"

Chad looked slightly embarrassed, but Luke

glanced at Stevie over his shoulder as he hoisted a case himself. "Don't worry, Officer, it's all legal," he drawled. "I turned twenty-one last spring."

"Whatever." Stevie had just been teasing—she already knew that Luke was a year or two older than her brother. She headed toward the house, panting a little under the weight of the beer. Phil picked up a box of sodas and followed. "So where do you want us to put all this stuff?" Stevie called back to Chad. "I don't want it in the living room—we still have to move the furniture around for the party."

"Let's stick a couple of cases of the beer in the spare fridge in the garage," Chad suggested, catching up to her on the front walk. "We'll want some to be cold when we get to our party."

"No way," Stevie countered. "You can't use that. Alex and Lisa and I spent all afternoon yesterday clearing it out so we could keep soda cold for *our* party." The extra refrigerator her parents kept in the garage wasn't very large, and Stevie was already worried about having enough cold drinks on hand for all the guests she had invited. She wanted all the partyers to be as happy and relaxed as possible so that they'd be easier marks for Scott's campaigning.

Chad frowned. "Come on, Stevie," he said.

"You can put your stuff in there after we leave tomorrow. What's the big deal?"

Before Stevie could argue back, Luke spoke up. "I've got a plan," he announced, catching up to the others. "Chad and I were going to pick up some big bags of ice on the way to our party tomorrow. What do you say we go a little earlier and get some extra for you guys? That way you can set up your sodas in the sink or the bathtub or wherever, and they'll stay cold."

"Hmmm." Stevie had to admit, at least to herself, that it was a good idea. She would be able to fit a lot more soda in the laundry room and kitchen sinks than she could possibly cram into the spare refrigerator, and it would be more convenient for her guests, too. She glanced at Phil, who nodded slightly, obviously guessing what she was thinking. "Well, okay," she told Chad and Luke. "I guess that would do. You can use a couple of shelves in the garage fridge, I guess."

"Cool." Chad looked relieved. "Come on, let's just get everything in from the car first. Then we can put stuff away." Shooting Stevie a quick glance, he added, "Don't worry, whatever doesn't go in the garage we'll stack in the dining room, so it won't be in your way."

"Okay." Stevie led the way into the house and

set the case she was carrying on the floor next to the box of sodas Chad had brought in earlier. She rubbed her arms and kicked at a bright red balloon that had escaped from the living room into the hall.

Luke noticed what she was doing and stepped past her to glance curiously into the living room. "Wow," he commented, taking in the inflated balloons drifting around the floor and the piles of red, white, and blue streamers waiting to be hung. "How old did you say you were, Stevie?"

Stevie felt almost annoyed enough to take back her agreement about the spare refrigerator. But then she shrugged. What did she care what Luke thought of her party decorations?

By this time tomorrow, Chad and Luke and Luke's skanky car full of beer will be long gone, she reminded herself. *Then the real fun can begin!*

"She's going to be all right, isn't she?" Lisa said anxiously, reaching over the stall door and running a hand down Prancer's neck.

"Try not to worry," Alex said comfortingly, putting his arm around Lisa's shoulders. "Max said Judy's coming back in a day or two for another look, right?"

Lisa nodded, smiling slightly as Prancer swung her big head around to look at Alex, almost knocking him over in the process. "She's going to stop by sometime over the weekend." Her smile faded and she sighed with frustration. "I just wish she'd been able to tell us something definite about her condition." Judy Barker had come to check on Prancer that morning while Lisa was in school, but according to Max, the vet had been unable to provide a definitive answer about the second foal and could only promise to check again soon.

"I know. It's tough being in suspense." Alex patted the mare on the cheek. "But no news is good news, right?"

"Well . . ." Lisa couldn't quite bring herself to agree with that old chestnut, not only because it wasn't necessarily true in Prancer's case, but also because it made her think about the secrets still standing between her and Alex. Telling Carole the other day about her conversation with Skye had lifted some of the guilt off her heart, but only temporarily. Every time she remembered all the things that she still hadn't told Alex about her summer, she felt like the world's worst girlfriend.

No news may be good news, but sometimes that makes things even worse when the bad news finally comes, she thought glumly, wishing once again that she'd been completely honest with Alex as soon as she'd returned from California. Every day that passed made it harder and harder to tell him, until she began to wonder whether she would ever be able to tell him at all.

Lisa had spent a lot of time over the past two months looking for the right moment to tell Alex that she had almost decided to stay in California for the school year instead of returning at the end of the summer. That had seemed like the hardest thing in the world to tell her boyfriend, who had been devastated even at the thought of spending two months apart.

She wasn't sure when her second secret had risen up and overtaken the other in her worries, but lately Lisa couldn't seem to stop thinking about that odd, slightly awkward conversation she and Skye had had in that faraway tack room. *When we first met you were what—twelve? Thirteen?* Skye had said seriously, gazing at her steadily with his striking ocean blue eyes. *Too young for a cool teenager like I was then to even consider as, well, you know. No matter how cute you were. Somehow, though, a few years' difference in our ages just doesn't seem that important anymore. . . .*

Lisa hadn't really known how to respond to that, but fortunately Skye hadn't expected her to say anything in return. He certainly hadn't expected her to stop being in love with Alex. He had just wanted her to know how he felt.

I almost wish he hadn't said anything, Lisa thought, glancing at her boyfriend out of the corner of her eye. *Then I wouldn't have one more secret to keep from Alex.* She knew that one of the reasons Alex hadn't wanted her to go to California for the summer was that he was jealous of her friendship with Skye. No matter how many times Lisa had reassured him that even a handsome, wealthy, successful movie star could never replace him in her heart, Alex had refused to be completely satisfied until she had finally returned home.

Alex didn't notice her contemplative expression—or if he did, he obviously attributed it to Prancer's condition. "I know what we need right now," he announced, reaching out to brush a strand of honey blond hair off her cheek. "Distraction. We need to take your mind off all the things that could be wrong before you give yourself an ulcer. Why don't we stop bugging this poor horse"—he patted Prancer again—"and go find something fun to do to keep you from worrying?"

Lisa turned away from the stall and gave him a hug, grateful as always at the way he often understood her feelings even better than she did herself. "That sounds like a good idea," she agreed. "We could go for a ride if you want. Or we could hang out at your house."

"Forget that second idea," Alex joked. "If I know my sister, she's probably right in the middle of some huge, elaborate party-planning frenzy right about now." He glanced at his watch. "Poor Chad is probably there by now, sorting Stevie's CD pile into alphabetical order or something while she cracks the whip."

Lisa smiled weakly. "Well, normally I'd say we could go to my house. But Mom is off this afternoon, so . . ."

She didn't bother to go into detail, since Alex already knew the reason she preferred to avoid her own house as much as possible these days when her mother was home. *Ever since I found out that Mom's seeing Rafe, that's all she wants to talk to me about,* she thought grimly. *And that long-haired loser is the last thing I feel like discussing.*

Lisa had been shocked when she had walked into her house two weeks earlier and found her mother—her conservative, recently divorced, forty-something mother—locked in a steamy embrace with a handsome twenty-four-year-old coworker. Mrs. Atwood had been embarrassed at first, but overall she'd seemed relieved to be found out and had soon begun confiding some of her feelings to her daughter.

It's totally disgusting. I mean, he's Peter's age! Lisa told herself, thinking of her older brother, who was living in Europe. *And the worst part is, Mom doesn't even seem to notice that I'm not as thrilled as she is about her exciting new boy toy.* . . .

In a way, that was the worst part. Lisa wouldn't have objected to her mother's starting to date again if she'd chosen almost anyone but Rafe. In fact, she would have welcomed it. Mrs. Atwood had been shattered by her divorce and had spent far too long feeling bitter and depressed and lonely. Lisa would have been honestly happy about anything that lifted her mother's spirits a little.

But not Rafe. Lisa could not get used to having him in her mother's life, no matter how many times Mrs. Atwood gushed about his interesting opinions about world events or his witty comments and great sense of humor or the way he flattered the customers at the clothing store where they both worked and convinced them to buy more. Not wanting to hear any more than she had to, Lisa had taken to avoiding her own home as much as possible whenever her mother might be there, doing most of her studying at the library or at Alex's house.

"Did I tell you the latest?" she asked Alex. "In the past couple of days, Mom has actually started hinting about having a big Thanksgiving celebration 'at home this year.' She pretends she means she just wants to invite Aunt Marianne and her family down, but I know what she's thinking." She shook her head grimly. "Especially since she's also mentioned several times that Rafe's family is in Seattle and he can't afford airfare home for both Thanksgiving *and* Christmas."

"Ick," Alex commented succinctly, wrinkling his nose. Then he brightened. "Hey, but you know what that means. It's all the more reason you and your mom should spend Thanksgiving at my house like we talked about."

Lisa hesitated, not sure what to say. She hadn't told Alex yet that her father had offered to fly her out to California to spend Thanksgiving with him. Whenever she imagined sitting around the table in his sunny kitchen, talking and laughing with her dad and Evelyn, helping to feed baby Lily her first bites of Thanksgiving turkey, she was tempted to accept the offer. Especially when the only other option seemed to be gritting her teeth and trying to choke down her food as her mother and Rafe made goo-goo eyes at each other while playing footsie under the table.

But I have a third option, she reminded herself. *I can stay here and spend a nice, romantic Thanksgiving with Alex. That way I don't have to deal with icky Rafe—Mom wouldn't dare invite him to the Lakes' house—and I also don't have to find a way to tell Alex I'm leaving again so soon. And I know Dad would understand. . . .*

That third option seemed a whole lot easier than either of the other possibilities. Knowing that she sometimes tended to overanalyze decisions, Lisa decided to commit before she could reason herself into changing her mind yet again.

"Okay," she told Alex, reaching over and squeezing his hand as they stood in the aisle outside Prancer's stall. "You talked me into it. I'll come to your house for Thanksgiving, as long as your parents say it's all right."

Alex's eyes lit up. "They will," he said eagerly. "Actually, they already have. I ran the idea past them last week." He shrugged and grinned. "So the only one you'll have to break the news to is Stevie. And as long as you don't try to steal the drumstick from her—"

"Hey, guys," Carole's voice interrupted.

Lisa turned and saw her friend approaching, weighted down by the pair of water buckets she was carrying. "Hi!" Lisa said. "I was looking for you before. Did Judy tell you any more about Prancer than she told Max?"

As Carole reached her friends and stopped to chat, lowering her buckets to the aisle floor, she couldn't help thinking, for the umpteenth time in the past two days, that she might never look at Lisa quite the same way again. Weird images kept popping into her head, especially when Lisa was with Alex. Images of Skye.

Alex had put his arm around his girlfriend's shoulders as the two of them turned to talk to Carole, but Carole didn't really see him there. Instead she pictured Skye Ransom, holding Lisa possessively as the two of them posed for the photographers at a fancy Hollywood premiere. *What would it be like, having a movie star in love with you?* she wondered. *Especially if he also happened to be a wonderful, caring person like Skye . . .*

Carole liked Alex. She thought he was good for Lisa and Lisa was good for him. Still, she couldn't help wondering—was Lisa really so devoted to Alex that she hadn't even considered what Skye could offer her? Had she thought about it all?

It's no wonder things are still a little tense between her and Alex, with those sorts of questions to deal with, she thought idly. *He must have totally freaked out when she first told him. Oh well. I'm just glad I wasn't around to witness it. . . .*

"Anyway," Lisa was saying after running down her usual list of fears and concerns for Prancer's health, "I think Alex and I are going to go for a quick trail ride. Can you let Max know when you see him?"

"Sure. Why don't you take out Barq and Congo? Neither of them has been exercised yet today." Even as she automatically came up with horse assignments, Carole's thoughts wandered away from thoughts of her friends and their problems straight back to her favorite topic: Samson.

I really ought to do some more hill work with him today, she thought, hardly listening as Lisa mentioned something about Stevie and tomorrow night's party. *He'll need to be strong for the show. He's not a novice horse, but he hasn't been in many really big shows. Most of the other horses will have a lot more experience than he does, so I'll have to make sure he's in absolute peak condition if we're going to have a chance at any ribbons. Maybe tomorrow we can—*

"Carole!" Her thoughts were interrupted by Lisa's voice, which sounded rather sharp. "Are you listening?"

"Sorry," Carole said immediately, feeling herself blush as she realized she'd drifted off completely on the current of her own thoughts and plans. "Um, I guess I'm a little distracted today. What did you say?"

Lisa seemed mollified by her apology. "Alex just asked if you knew whether Ben was coming to the party. I know Stevie invited him."

Carole's first impulse was to say that she was the last person who would know what Ben was up to these days. But she held back. She didn't want her friends to know how strange and complicated their relationship had gotten lately.

She had never really understood Ben very well, but she'd always thought he respected her for the work she did at the stable. Lately, though, she wasn't so sure about that. Ben had started looking at her strangely at times, making cryptic little comments. . . . The previous weekend the two of them had actually ended up in a tense argument, even though Carole wasn't even sure exactly what they'd been fighting about.

Still, the next time she'd seen him, Ben hadn't acted any differently toward her at all, and there hadn't been much time for silly awkwardness between them for the past week—especially not when they were both busy keeping an extra-vigilant eye on Prancer in addition to all their other duties at the stable. But when the mysterious young stable hand wasn't actually present, Carole couldn't help feeling a little uncomfortable every time she thought about him.

"Um, I don't know," she told Lisa. "I sort of doubt it. He's not exactly the social type, in case you haven't noticed."

"Well, remind him about the party when you see him, okay?" Alex said. "Stevie seems to think he might come if you ask him."

What does Stevie mean by that? Carole wondered briefly. But she quickly brushed the thought away, figuring that Stevie probably just meant that she talked to Ben more than anybody else.

"Okay. I'll remind him," she told Alex and Lisa. "I'd better get back to work. Have a nice ride."

As her friends headed for the tack room, Carole picked up her water buckets again with a slight groan. Lisa and Alex's talk had started her thinking about tomorrow's party. Part of her wished it could be held another weekend—she had so much to do before the horse show that she wasn't sure how she was going to get it all done in time. Taking a whole evening out to go to a party when she could be at the stable, working with Samson or catching up on chores, seemed almost ridiculously frivolous.

Still, there's no way I'm going to miss Emily's last hurrah, she reminded herself. *Besides, I guess I deserve a little fun, especially after everything I've been through lately. . . .*

She was thinking of her aching arms hoisting the water buckets, but her thoughts were turned by a quick stab of guilt as she remembered something that had happened a few weeks earlier. Carole had spent so much time at Pine Hollow one weekend that she'd completely forgotten to study for a history test and had flunked it in a big way. Her teacher had agreed to a retest after Carole, desperate at the thought of losing her riding privileges—Max insisted that all his riders maintain a C average or better—had made up a story about her father being ill. But Carole had found herself no better prepared the second time around than she'd been the first, and when her teacher had left the room for a few minutes, she'd peeked at the answers in her textbook. Ever since, the incident had gnawed at her, popping into her mind at odd times and making her feel guiltier than she'd ever felt about anything in her life.

She tried to remind herself that if she hadn't done what she'd done, there was no way she would be getting ready to ride in the Colesford Horse Show in a couple of weeks. And that was something she didn't like to think about at all. She couldn't wait for the moment when she and Samson stepped into the ring, when he got his chance to show everyone how talented he was. . . .

It will all be worth it, she told herself stubbornly. *All of it.*

THREE

Lisa leaned closer to the mirror over her dresser, blinking and checking for smudges in the mascara she'd just applied. She rarely wore much makeup, recognizing that her delicate features and ivory complexion called for a light touch, but she was taking extra care with the little she did wear tonight. She wanted to look her best for the party. Picking up her favorite berry-tinted lip gloss, she applied it carefully and then took a step back to examine her reflection, moving her eyes from her face down to the stylish midnight blue cashmere sweater she was wearing. Finally satisfied with her appearance, she dropped her lip gloss into her small purse and headed for the bedroom door.

Time to get into the party mood, she thought, wondering whether she would be able to do it. She hadn't learned anything new about Prancer—Judy had been busy at another stable all day and hadn't been able to check on the mare again—and Lisa thought that if she had to wait another whole day to find out more, she might explode. On top of that, while accepting Alex's invitation to Thanksgiving dinner had made her feel better for a little while, ultimately it had just made her feel even worse about the secrets she was still keeping from him. Still, she was determined to forget about all that for one night if she possibly could. Emily's family was moving in three days, and this would be Lisa's last chance to spend any time with her old friend. She didn't want to let anything ruin that.

When she reached the bottom of the stairs, she found her mother waiting for her. One look at her mother's jittery expression and too-bright smile and Lisa knew that something was going on. When she took in Mrs. Atwood's outfit—a short, form-fitting jersey dress more suited to someone Lisa's age—Lisa guessed that Rafe was involved.

"Oh, don't you look lovely!" Mrs. Atwood exclaimed when she caught sight of her daughter. "That sweater is so perfect on you."

"Thanks, Mom," Lisa said. "I'm going to head over to the Lakes' now. I promised Stevie and Alex that I'd come a little early and help them set up."

"That's fine, dear," Mrs. Atwood replied brightly. She winked and leaned a little closer. "I have some special plans tonight myself. Rafe's coming over, and we—"

"That's great," Lisa interrupted, her voice a little too loud. Why couldn't her mother see how uncomfortable she was discussing Rafe? She didn't think she was particularly good at hiding it. Every time she thought about Rafe, she remembered catching him making out with her mother. Recalling that unpleasant little scene still gave her the heebie-jeebies, and she couldn't help wishing, irrational as it was, that the whole Rafe problem would just go away. That didn't seem likely to happen anytime soon, so all she could do was continue to try to limit her exposure to him and hope that her mother came to her senses someday. Of course, she also needed to tell her mother that Alex had invited them to Thanksgiving dinner before Mrs. Atwood did anything stupid, like actually inviting Rafe to share a turkey with them.

No time like the present, right? Lisa thought, gazing at her mother and willing herself to bring up the topic. But she wasn't sure she could manage the energy for that particular discussion at that moment, so soon before the party. Especially when Rafe himself could arrive and interrupt them at any moment. *Oh well,* she thought. *I guess it can wait one more day. I'll just make sure to tell her tomorrow before she leaves for work.*

"Okay," she said, grabbing her light corduroy jacket out of the hall closet and pulling it on over her dress. "Well, I guess I'd better—"

The phone rang, cutting her off. Mrs. Atwood stepped across the hall to answer the extension just inside the living room. Her voice was bright as she answered, but as soon as she heard who was at the other end of the line, her expression tightened.

"It's for you," she told Lisa, holding out the receiver as if she'd suddenly noticed it was actually a scorpion. "Your father."

"Thanks." Lisa hurried to grab the phone. "Hello? Dad?"

"Hi, sweetie. How's it going?"

"Great." Lisa glanced at her watch. "Um, so what's up?"

Her father's familiar laugh came through the line. "Do I need a reason to call my own daughter?"

"Sorry." Lisa smiled and pressed the phone closer to her ear. "It's just that Stevie and Alex are having a party tonight, and I was just on my way out. . . ."

"Say no more," her father said immediately.

"I won't keep you. I was really just calling to see if you'd made up your mind about Thanksgiving yet. Evelyn and I are really hoping you'll decide to come out here. We'd love to see you."

Lisa bit her lip. "Um, I'm not sure yet," she lied, not ready to break the news to him about spending the holiday with Alex. *I'll call him tomorrow, after I talk to Mom, when I have time to explain,* she promised herself. "I'll let you know soon, okay?"

"Okay. Have fun tonight."

"Thanks." Lisa heaved a deep sigh as she hung up. Her mother had pointedly left the room after handing her the phone, so Lisa was alone when she reentered the hallway.

Time to make my escape, she thought, grabbing her purse off the chair where she'd dropped it. Pausing just long enough to check her reflection in the small decorative mirror on the wall near the door, she spun, pulled the door open, and hurried through it.

She stopped short on the threshold, just in time to keep from crashing into Rafe, who was standing on the doorstep with his hand raised, poised to knock.

"Whoa," he said, his full lips stretching with mild amusement at her startled face. "Where's the fire?"

"Hello, Rafe," Lisa greeted him carefully. She found herself shuddering as she caught a whiff of his musky cologne, which he seemed to have applied with a garden hose, and noticed that he was carrying a bottle of wine. Obviously he'd come prepared for an evening of major romance and minor subtlety.

Lisa tried not to think about what that meant as she dodged around him, making a hasty exit. Once she was safely down the front path, she paused to take a few deep breaths of the cool early-evening air and forced herself to relax before heading across the yard in the direction of the Lakes' house. *Tonight's going to be fun,* she thought. *And nothing—not even Mom's sudden insanity—is going to spoil it.*

"Lisa's here," Alex called from the front hall.

Stevie hardly glanced up from the snacks she was arranging on the long table she'd set up in front of the living room fireplace. She'd been busy getting the house ready for the party since early that morning, and now that the zero hour was rapidly approaching, she wanted to make sure everything was perfect. "Hi, Lisa!" she called back automatically.

"Hi." Lisa came into the room, glancing around at the decorations as she shrugged off her jacket. "Looks good in here." She dropped her purse and coat on a handy chair. "So what can I do to help?"

"Keep my hyper brother occupied," Stevie replied, only half kidding. She gestured at Alex, who had come into the room on Lisa's heels. "He's been driving me nuts all afternoon."

Lisa smiled and wrapped both arms around Alex's waist. "Easy enough," she said, standing on tiptoes to kiss him on the ear. Leaving her arms around him, she glanced at Stevie. "Where's Phil?"

"Coming later." Stevie gave her friend a meaningful look. "With A.J."

"Really?"

Lisa sounded surprised, and Stevie didn't blame her. She'd been amazed herself when Phil had called earlier to report that he would be playing chauffeur for A. J. McDonnell and his girlfriend, Julianna. Phil and A.J. had been best friends for years, but just the week before they'd had a fight that Stevie, for one, wasn't sure they'd ever get over. It had all started when A.J. had discovered, purely by accident, that he was adopted. He hadn't been planning to tell his parents that he knew, but Phil had told, and A.J. had been furious.

"Really," Stevie confirmed. "I guess Julianna

was behind it—she arranged a sort of truce between them. Don't ask me how. All I know is that they're all coming over here together a little later."

"Wow. Big news." Lisa shook her head slowly.

Stevie shoved aside a bowl of peanuts to make more room for a stack of napkins that was hanging half off the edge of the table. "Speaking of news, is there any about Prancer? I didn't get over to Pine Hollow at all today."

"Nothing new," Lisa said, worry creeping onto her face. "Judy's going to try to stop by tomorrow and check again."

"Well, I guess all we can do until then is wait." Rubbing her stomach absently, Stevie stepped back from the snack table and looked Lisa over. "Hey, by the way, you look great. Awesome sweater."

"Thanks. Are you all right?" Lisa asked. "Is your stomach bothering you or something?"

"Not really." Stevie waved one hand dismissively. "I guess I'm just a little hungry, that's all. I didn't really have time to eat dinner."

"Not unless you consider a candy bar and a handful of popcorn dinner," Alex put in, grabbing a cookie out of a bowl on the table.

Stevie slapped his hand. "Stop that, you pig,"

she ordered briskly. "I don't want all the food gone before the guests start arriving."

As if on cue, the doorbell rang. "I'll get it," Lisa offered, hurrying off toward the entryway. A moment later she returned, followed by Scott and Callie Forester.

"Hi, guys," Stevie said, glad to see them. Scott had promised to arrive early—partly to help with final party prep, but mostly so he wouldn't miss a moment of time he could spend campaigning. *Cool,* she thought. *Looks like Veronica didn't manage to bum a ride over with him. Maybe she finally got the hint.*

Scott's handsome face wore his usual easygoing smile. "Hey, we heard there was a party here," he said. "We came to crash it."

Meanwhile, Callie was glancing around the room, looking surprised at all the patriotic decorations. "Wow, this place looks like one of Dad's postelection victory parties," she commented. Leaning on her crutches, she slipped out of the denim jacket she was wearing over slim black pants and a cashmere sweater. "Is that supposed to be some kind of statement on Emily's departure from the good old U.S. of A.?"

"Oh, um—sure," Stevie said. "That'll work." She reached out to take Callie's jacket. "Anyway, thanks for coming early. You two look great."

She had checked Scott's appearance first, making sure that he'd worn the conservative cotton sweater and khaki pants she'd decided would best fit the mature but approachable image she wanted him to project at this party. His wavy hair was brushed back neatly, and he looked as solid and handsome as always.

When she turned her attention to Callie, Stevie noted that she, too, had paid a little extra attention to her appearance for the party. Callie was always beautiful, with her long, smooth blond hair and her flawless face. But tonight, with her hair caught at the crown of her head in a pair of sparkly barrettes and a touch of pale gray shadow highlighting her intense indigo eyes, she looked downright stunning.

George is probably going to flip his lid when he gets a load of Callie tonight, Stevie thought, her mind wandering back to the evening the week before when George Wheeler, a classmate of hers and Callie's and a fellow rider at Pine Hollow, had confessed to Stevie that he was interested in Callie as more than a friend. Stevie wasn't sure how to feel about that knowledge. She hadn't said anything to Callie, mostly because she was pretty sure that Callie wouldn't return George's feelings. He was a nice enough guy, smart in school and an excellent rider, but he was also short and stocky and moon-faced, awkward with girls and shy and bumbling in social situations. *Hardly the kind of stud muffin to sweep Callie off her feet,* Stevie thought ruefully.

She pushed those thoughts out of her head. There was still plenty of work to do in the hour remaining before George and the rest of the world started arriving. "Okay," she said briskly. "Chad should be here soon with the ice, and then we can—"

"Stevie!" Chad's voice called from the hall. "Alex! Get out here and help us carry. This ice weighs a ton!"

"Keep your shirt on!" Stevie called back. She glanced at Scott, Alex, and Lisa. "Ready for a little exercise?"

Scott struck a pose, flexing his biceps like a bodybuilder. "Lead the way," he replied with a grin.

Callie drifted along behind the others, even though she knew that with her crutches, she wouldn't be good for much more than holding the door. When she reached the front hall, she saw that Stevie's older brother wasn't alone.

Callie found her gaze drawn instantly to Chad's friend, a lean, tall, edgily good-looking guy with sleek dark hair and a hint of stubble on his chin. His eyes, which were narrow and icy blue, met her own with frank curiosity and a hint of a challenge.

"Hi there," he said, lowering the bag of ice he was holding to the floor, taking a step toward her, and running his eyes casually up and down her body, hardly seeming to notice the metal crutches. "I'm Luke. And you are?"

"Callie Forester," Callie replied as coolly as she could, feeling a little thrill at the obvious admiration in Luke's eyes. "Nice to meet you."

Chad glanced at his friend. "Hey, watch it, man," he complained, balancing a large bag of ice on each broad shoulder. "Don't leave that bag on the floor. If it leaks on the hardwood, Mom and Dad will freak."

"I'll get it." Scott stepped forward to retrieve Luke's bag, slinging it easily over one shoulder.

Callie was glad. Luke was still holding her gaze with his own, and somehow she didn't want him to stop. She hardly noticed as Scott and Chad headed down the hall with their bags while Stevie, Alex, and Lisa trooped out through the front door on their way to the car.

"You must be the girl who was in the car accident this summer, right?" Luke said, taking another step closer so that he was close enough to touch. "Chad told me about that. Bad luck."

"Yeah." Callie was glad she didn't have to explain about her crutches. "So you go to college with Chad?" She found herself wishing that she'd paid more attention to Stevie's older brother the few times they'd met. If he hung out with guys like Luke up at college, it might be worth her while to get to know him better.

Luke ran one hand through his dark hair and shrugged. "Yeah, I'm a senior at NVU. Econ and prelaw."

"Cool." Callie felt a little breathless, unable to say much more. She couldn't remember the last time she'd had this sort of instant physical reaction to a guy. Not since her accident, or maybe even longer—since before her family had moved to Willow Creek.

Chad returned at that moment, mopping his brow and shooting Luke a slightly sour look. "Come on," he said. "It was your idea to bring all that extra ice for the young 'uns, remember?"

"In a minute." Luke still hadn't taken his eyes off Callie, though he was speaking to Chad. "I'm starting to think maybe this bachelor party is going to be kind of lame. Who wants to go to a party with a bunch of guys when there are gorgeous girls to hang with right here?"

Callie blushed as Chad rolled his eyes and headed for the door to help Stevie, who was staggering in under the weight of two large bags of ice. "Too bad you can't stay," Callie told Luke, keeping her voice casual. "It should be fun."

"I'll bet." Luke's gaze was hungrier than ever as he reached out and ran a hand down her arm, from shoulder to elbow, making her skin tingle under her sleeve. "Lots of fun."

Chad was walking past again, heading down the hall to the kitchen, but he paused and gave Callie a worried glance before continuing on his way. Callie didn't pay much attention to him. She was too busy trying to figure out what to say next to keep Luke interested. *I'm getting rusty,* she thought in dismay. *It's been so long since a cool guy gave me the time of day that I've almost forgotten what it's like.*

"So listen," Luke said, leaning a little closer. "Callie. Do you think you might be coming up to visit Chad with Stevie anytime soon? Because I—"

"Luke." Chad had returned just in time to interrupt his friend. "Listen, man. I'm serious. Get your butt out to the car and help carry in the last few bags, or we're going to be late. Remember, we've still got to move all our ice from your car to Mom's if you want me to drive tonight."

Luke shot his friend an annoyed glance, then sighed. "Yeah, yeah, okay," he said, sounding a bit irritable. "I'll go get the damn ice, okay?" He rubbed Callie's arm again lightly. "Don't go anywhere, okay, beautiful? I'll be right back."

"Sure." Callie shivered with anticipation as she watched him turn and lope toward the door, leaving her alone in the hall with Chad.

"Callie." Chad's voice was serious. "Listen, I feel like I ought to say something here. I mean, it's pretty obvious that Luke is into you."

"Really?" Callie tried to act casual, though she couldn't help smiling. "You think? He seems pretty cool."

Chad glanced toward the door, then gestured for Callie to follow him into the quiet, empty dining room. She did so, feeling intrigued.

"Okay," Chad said when they were inside, running one hand over his handsome but worried face. "Here's the deal. I don't know you that well, and I don't want to come across as, like, some kind of busybody. But I just think you should know what you're getting into with Luke. He's kind of bad news."

"I thought he was your friend."

"He is." Chad shrugged, looking slightly sheepish. "I'm not saying he's all bad, you know? It's just that he has kind of a history when it comes to women. He's a love-'em-and-leave-'em kind of guy."

Callie bit back a smile, thinking about everything she'd ever heard from Stevie and the others about Chad's own dating history. According to all reports, he'd made a habit of dating a different girl just about every week from the age of fourteen on. *You're one to talk, loverboy,* she thought with amusement. But she didn't say anything, since Chad still looked very serious and concerned.

"Really." Chad's voice was earnest. "I mean— Look, Callie, you're a big girl. You can do whatever you want about Luke. But I just thought you should know what you were getting into. He's always really attentive and everything at first, but as soon as the girl starts getting into it, really liking him, he dumps her. Not usually in the nicest way, either."

Callie couldn't help frowning a little at that. She could take care of herself, but maybe Chad had a point. Right now, with everything else that was going on in her life, it might not be such a good idea to get involved with someone like Luke.

"Thanks, Chad," she said, meaning it. "I get your point. And I appreciate it."

Chad nodded, looking relieved. "Good." He patted her on the shoulder and smiled. "Sorry if I came across like the date police there."

"You didn't," Callie assured him, returning his smile. "Thanks again."

It was nice of him to warn me, she thought as the two of them returned to the hallway. Luke was just entering with a large bag of ice. *He didn't have to do that. And he was so cool about it, too—he didn't lecture me like Dad would, or even Scott.*

Luke spotted them and shifted the ice from one arm to the other. "This is the last bag of theirs," he told Chad. "What should I do with it?"

"Take it into the kitchen," Chad directed. "Stevie and the others are there setting up."

Luke nodded, then shifted his gaze to Callie. "Want to come along?" he asked. "Keep me company?"

"I'll be in in a minute." Callie kept her voice completely neutral this time, figuring that it wasn't a good idea to encourage him anymore. "I've got to take care of some other stuff first."

Luke obviously got the message. He looked surprised, then annoyed. "Whatever," he muttered, heading down the hall.

Callie watched him go, feeling a pang of regret. He really was awfully sexy. . . . But when she saw Chad shoot her a quick wink and a thumbs-up before following his buddy toward the kitchen, she felt a little better immediately. Meeting a hot guy who was interested in her looks was one thing, but it was a lot rarer to find out that someone she barely knew seemed interested in being a real friend.

FOUR

"**S**he's here!" Stevie cried, rushing into the living room half an hour later. "Hey, everyone, listen up! Emily's here. So get ready!"

Carole glanced up from the cup of soda she'd just poured out of one of the bottles in the kitchen sink. "I guess we'd better get out there," she told Lisa, who was standing beside her munching on a cookie.

Lisa giggled. "Right. Time to sing. Let's just hope Emily has strong ears."

Carole smiled as the two of them hurried toward the living room. Stevie had arranged things so that Emily would arrive a little later than everyone else, and in the meantime she'd insisted that all the guests practice a little farewell song she'd composed especially for Emily. It was set to the tune of "Jingle Bells" and was rather grandly entitled "Fond Farewells: An Ode to Emily upon her Departure for Australia." Carole, for one, still wasn't sure she would remember all the complicated lyrics when the time came—especially the verse that rhymed "we'll miss you" and "didgeridoo"—but she was willing to try, for Emily's sake as well as to keep Stevie happy. And she was sure Emily would appreciate the effort.

Emily did. Her face lit up as soon as she entered the living room and saw the crowd gathered to greet her. "Hi, everyone!" she exclaimed, waving one of her crutches merrily. Emily had been born with cerebral palsy and could get around only with the aid of crutches, a wheelchair or a horse, though she hadn't let that stop her from enjoying a full life and making plenty of friends, as evidenced by the welcoming calls that greeted her entrance from all sides.

"Welcome, Emily!" Stevie cried dramatically, stepping to the front of the group and quickly helping Emily off with her jacket. Then she turned to face the room and waved her arms for quiet. "All right, everyone. Don't we all have something we want to say—or, to be precise, sing?"

On that cue, everyone launched into a slightly ragged but enthusiastic rendition of Stevie's masterpiece. Or almost everyone, anyway. As she sang at the top of her lungs, Carole suddenly noticed that there was one person in the room who didn't seem to be participating. Ben Marlow was hanging back near the edge of the group, looking uncomfortable and hardly bothering to pretend to mumble along.

What's wrong with him? Carole thought with an uncharacteristic flash of annoyance at him. *Why did he bother to come to this party if he doesn't even care enough about Emily to pretend to have a good time?*

She had been surprised when he'd arrived in the first place. When she'd mentioned the party to him that morning as she'd promised Lisa she would, she'd expected him to mutter an excuse for not being able to go. Instead, he'd merely nodded at the reminder and accepted her offer of a ride over from the stable.

I guess he's just full of surprises, she thought with a shrug, returning her attention to the guest of honor. Fortunately Emily didn't seem to have noticed Ben and was clapping along enthusiastically, laughing at the silly lyrics, her open, friendly face glowing with happiness. Everyone except Ben was clearly having a wonderful time, from Stevie and Alex and Lisa, to Scott and Callie Forester, to Veronica diAngelo and the gaggle of friends she'd brought with her. Carole estimated that there were at least thirty-five people at the party already—people from Willow Creek High School, from Pine Hollow, from Fenton Hall, and even from Cross County High School, where Phil went.

It's nice that everyone turned out to see Emily off like this, Carole thought, humming along as the others hit a verse involving a description of the differences between a crocodile and a horse, the words to which she'd completely forgotten. *When you're about to do something really hard, like moving to another continent, it always helps to know that your friends wish you well.*

Stevie perched on the arm of the living room sofa and glanced anxiously at her watch. Her song had gone over better than she'd hoped, and even now, fifteen minutes later, people kept stopping by to congratulate her on her lyrical talents. Still, she couldn't manage to enjoy it completely, not when Phil still hadn't arrived.

I hope A.J. didn't decide to hijack the car on the way over here and drive off to Mexico or something, she thought, only half kidding. Maybe A.J. hadn't resorted to anything as dramatic as kidnapping quite yet, but the way he'd changed since finding out about his adoption made Stevie ready to believe he'd be capable of almost anything. After all, if the kind, funny, sensitive guy she'd known for years could change overnight into a withdrawn, depressed, sullen jerk, who knew what else could happen?

Stevie knew she wasn't being totally fair. As difficult as A.J.'s crisis had been for his friends—especially Phil—to deal with lately, it was obvious that no one was suffering more than A.J. himself. Still, it was hard for her to watch A.J. constantly dump all over Phil, who was only doing his best to help.

That's probably why they're late, she realized, wandering over to the window to check the street outside for Phil's parents' car. *A.J. probably decided at the last minute to chicken out of coming to the party, and Phil's there trying to convince him to come and have a good time.*

She sighed, then did her best to smile as Nicole Adams, a classmate from Fenton Hall, came over to gush about the party. Stevie thanked her and then tactfully steered her toward the little clutch of people gathered around Scott, who was chatting casually about Fenton Hall's various student regulations. Stevie was happy to see that at least half a dozen of their schoolmates were hanging on his every word, although she felt a little less happy when she noticed that among that half dozen was Veronica diAngelo.

I'll have to take care of that situation after Phil

gets here, she decided. *If Veronica hangs around trying to distract Scott all night, he'll never get to talk to everyone.*

She glanced out the window again just in time to see a familiar station wagon pulling to the curb. "It's about time," she muttered, feeling relieved as she watched Phil, A.J., and Julianna climb out of the car. She hurried to the door to meet them, torn between eagerness to see Phil and a slight uneasiness as she wondered which personality A.J. would be wearing that evening.

"Hi!" she called as the trio came up the walk. "I thought you'd never get here."

"It was all Julianna's fault," A.J. called back with a grin. "She took so long putting on her makeup, I didn't think she'd be ready until Christmas."

Julianna stuck out her tongue at him playfully, and A.J. responded by grabbing her around the waist and carrying her the rest of the way up the walk as she giggled and struggled to escape, her silky red hair flying as she tossed her head.

I guess that means they're back together, Stevie thought as she greeted Phil with a quick kiss and then stood back to let the three newcomers enter. One of the first things A.J. had done after discovering that he was adopted was to break up with Julianna, who had been his girlfriend of several months. *I guess it also means that A.J. is actually in a partying mood—thank goodness.*

Phil glanced around as he entered the house, which was packed with people, overflowing from the living room into the hallway, den, and kitchen. A few guests were even perched on the stairs, talking and sipping their sodas. The sounds of talk and laughter almost drowned out the dance music Stevie had put on the stereo, although a few people, including Lisa and Alex, were already dancing in a clear area in the middle of the living room.

"Wow," Phil commented. "I have to hand it to you, Stevie. You really know how to throw a party."

"Was there ever any doubt?" Stevie teased, putting an arm around his waist.

"Phil! A.J.! Julianna!" Emily exclaimed, spotting them and swinging toward them on her crutches. "I'm glad you came."

"Sorry we're late," Phil replied, stepping forward to give Emily a hug.

"Better late than never," she responded cheerfully.

A.J. leaped forward, pushed Phil aside, and planted a big kiss on Emily's cheek, almost knocking her crutches out from under her. "Say it isn't so, Emily!" he cried dramatically, making a goofy face. "Say you're not really leaving us for a bunch of kangaroos!"

Emily giggled and shoved him aside, grabbing Phil's arm for balance as she rearranged her crutches. "Sorry. I'm afraid it's true."

A.J. covered his face with his hands and pretended to sob. "No, no, nooooo!"

Julianna laughed loudly and grabbed A.J.'s arm, hugging it to her. "Hey, don't be too upset," she said breathlessly. "At least we get to party with her for one more night."

"Hey, you're right!" A.J. looked up quickly and grinned widely. Grabbing Julianna, he spun her around and did a quick little tango with her while she and Emily laughed.

Stevie felt slightly puzzled as she watched A.J. continue to kid around with Emily and the others. On the one hand, he was acting a lot more like the fun-loving, life-of-the-party guy he'd been before finding out about his adoption. But Stevie couldn't help thinking that it was really just an act. A.J. had always been funny and lively, but at the moment he seemed downright manic, almost as if being friendly was costing him a great deal of effort.

It's like he's trying to convince us—or himself, maybe—that he's back to normal, she thought, glancing over at Phil to see whether he was noticing the same thing she was. *But he's trying a little too hard.*

Phil met her eye and shrugged, making it clear that he had noticed. For the first time, Stevie realized that A.J. hadn't spoken to Phil or even looked at him since they'd arrived. That seemed to indicate that he hadn't forgiven him yet for spilling his secret to his parents, which Stevie guessed might also have something to do with the weird way he was acting.

He's probably just nervous, she told herself as A.J. picked up a squealing Emily and carried her off in the direction of the living room with Julianna trailing along behind carrying Emily's crutches. *This is his first big social appearance since his secret came out, and on top of it all he's not speaking to his best friend. That would be enough to put anyone on edge. He'll relax after a while.* She bit her lip as she caught a glimpse through the living room doorway of A.J. jumping onto the sofa and starting to dance, almost stepping on George Wheeler, who'd been sitting there. *I hope so, anyway.*

Half an hour later, Lisa's party mood was in full swing. Miraculously, she'd been able to keep her vow to forget her worries and have fun for one night. Banishing from her mind all thoughts

73

of Prancer's health, her mother's disturbing relationship with Rafe, her anxiety about Thanksgiving, and her own secret about Skye, she had joined in the festive mood of the people all around her. After Stevie's silly welcome song, Emily had been so mobbed with friends and well-wishers that Lisa hadn't been able to get near her, so she'd dragged Alex off to dance and they'd been having a great time ever since. Alex didn't share her natural grace on the dance floor, but he was enthusiastic, and that was enough for her.

Now she laughed out loud as he spun her around under his arm, almost sending her crashing into a group of Fenton Hall students who were dancing nearby, and then pulled her to him, holding her tight. "Stop," she protested happily. "You're all sweaty."

He hugged her tighter, rubbing his moist cheek against her own. "Is that a problem?"

Lisa pushed him away, still laughing. "You're a beast," she told him fondly, reaching up to push back a lock of his damp brown hair. "But I might forgive you for that if you go get me a soda."

"Your wish is my command, beautiful lady," he said, grabbing her hand and kissing it with a flourish before turning and pushing his way through the crowds in the direction of the kitchen.

Lisa was still laughing at his antics when she saw Gary Korman, a guy who was in several of her classes at school, wandering toward her, his tall, thin body bent as always in a slouch that made him look as if he'd just crawled out of bed and wasn't quite awake yet. "Hi, Gary," she greeted him, still breathless from dancing.

"Hey, Lisa," he replied, tossing his head to clear his long curly dark hair out of his eyes. "Pretty cool party, huh?"

She nodded, dodging just in time to avoid a flying arm as several girls she didn't know danced enthusiastically past her. "I can't believe so many people came," she said, glancing around at the crowds. Emily was standing near the doorway talking to George Wheeler, Polly Giacomin, and a couple of other Pine Hollow riders. Stevie and Phil were dancing nearby. A.J. was goofing off across the room with Julianna and some other friends. Scott Forester was leaning on the end of the sofa, talking animatedly with several schoolmates. Everyone seemed to be smiling and having a good time. And more people kept pouring in all the time, arriving singly, in pairs, or in larger groups and quickly melting into the noisy, active excitement of the party.

Gary blinked his large, soulful brown eyes. "Listen," he said. "I hate to be a downer on a night like tonight, but I have to ask. What result did you get in that physics lab yesterday? I'm afraid my group bombed it."

"It was a tricky one," Lisa admitted. "What we did was . . ."

She went on to describe the lab as she waited for Alex to return with her drink, swaying gently to the music as she talked with Gary. She couldn't remember the last time she'd felt so relaxed and happy.

At the same time, Carole felt a little giddy as she pushed her way through a shrieking knot of Fenton Hall girls on her way to the kitchen. A couple of friends from school had dragged her onto the dance floor soon after Emily's welcome song, and now she was exhausted. But she had to admit that she was having a fantastic time. Once she'd managed to stop worrying about Samson and all the work she wasn't getting done at Pine Hollow, she had found herself really getting into the spirit of the evening. Even Ben wasn't weighing much on her mind anymore, although the few times she'd spotted him lately he had looked just as grumpy and bored as he had earlier.

Too bad he can't lighten up for once, she

thought, moving aside to avoid a guy who seemed to be inventing some kind of bizarre interpretive dance all by himself in the living room doorway. *Maybe then he'd realize that this party is a total blast. I should try going to parties more often—at least once the Colesford show is over.*

She mopped her brow and hurried on down the hall, looking forward to downing one of the cold sodas Stevie had sunk into the ice filling the kitchen sink. When she entered the kitchen, she found George Wheeler standing in front of the sink talking to a classmate and drinking grape soda. "Hi," Carole said. "Is there any of that left?"

"Not in here," George said in his soft, tentative voice. "I snagged the last one. You could check the laundry tub."

Carole nodded and moved on, dodging a boy she didn't recognize, who had his head buried in the Lakes' refrigerator, where he seemed to be exploring the contents of the vegetable crisper. Soon she was hurrying down the short, narrow hallway leading to the small laundry room that separated the Lakes' garage from the rest of the house. She arrived just in time to see Alex reaching for the garage doorknob.

"Hey," she greeted him. "Where are you going?"

"Would you believe me if I said I was going out to wash my car?"

"Nope." Carole smiled. "Especially since Stevie claims you've never ever washed that car since you two got it."

"Okay, okay, you caught me. I guess I'll have to trust you with my secret." Alex smiled, put a finger to his lips, and then peered past her down the hallway as if making sure that no one could overhear. "Here it is. Lisa asked me to get her a drink. You know that flavored iced tea she likes so much?" Alex rubbed his hands together. "Well, I stashed a few bottles of it out in the garage fridge yesterday where nobody else would find it and drink it."

Carole giggled. "Pretty sneaky."

"Hey, what can I say? I'm an excellent boy-friend." Alex grinned. "Come on. If you promise not to give away my secret, I'll let you have one bottle from my stash."

"Okay." Carole didn't really care about the iced tea, but she followed him willingly, thinking it would feel good to get out into the cooler air in the garage for a few minutes.

The two of them chatted about Emily's move as they walked into the garage together. Alex flicked on the overhead light, then went straight to the half-sized refrigerator against the back wall.

"Okay, let's see now . . ." Alex swung open the door, then stopped short, looking surprised.

"What?" Carole asked. Her view of the refrigerator's interior was blocked by the door. She leaned over to peer inside. "Did someone find your—Whoa! Is that beer?"

Alex nodded slowly. "Chad stowed a couple of cases in here yesterday—I guess he forgot when he left for his party."

Carole wasn't quite sure what he was talking about. She hadn't even known that Chad was in town. But she just smiled nervously in response. "Hey, maybe you should bring Lisa one of those instead," she joked. "That would surprise her even more than the iced tea."

"Yeah, right." Alex laughed, then quickly grabbed a bottle of iced tea off the bottom shelf. "Come on, we'd better get back in there. Oh, take one if you want."

"A beer?" Carole laughed, still feeling a little nervous. She quickly grabbed an iced tea and slammed the refrigerator door shut. "Okay, let's go."

She followed Alex back into the laundry room and down the hall. Just before they reached the turn to the kitchen, Alex stopped and turned to face Carole. "Listen," he said. "We probably shouldn't—"

"I won't say a word," Carole promised immediately.

"Good." Alex looked relieved.

Carole didn't blame him. It made her more than a little apprehensive to know that all that beer was right outside in the garage where anyone could happen upon it, especially since Mr. and Mrs. Lake weren't home. *Still, it's not as if the people at this party are the type to go crazy just because there's beer around,* she thought as she trailed Alex through the kitchen, dodging a couple of guys who were having a food fight with the contents of the refrigerator. Carole wrinkled her nose and ducked as a wad of tuna salad sailed past her head, missing her by an inch. *Well, not most of them anyway. Besides, Stevie would probably throttle anyone who tried it.*

She was so busy smiling at that thought that she almost ran into Alex, who had stopped short again just ahead of her in the living room doorway. "Oops!" she said. "Sorry, I—What's wrong?" She'd just stepped around him and gotten a look at his face, which was grim and angry.

Alex didn't answer. He didn't even seem to have heard her. At first Carole thought he might be worried about the number of guests at the party—eight or ten more people were pouring into the front hall at the moment, dropping their jackets and purses here and there and throwing themselves immediately into the festivities. But when she followed his gaze past A.J. and Julianna, who were tangoing again, Carole realized that he was looking at Lisa, who was at the edge of the makeshift dance floor in the middle of the room, talking to Gary Korman. As Carole watched, Gary leaned a little closer, hunching his shoulders even more than usual as he bent to hear something Lisa was saying, resting one hand casually on her elbow.

"What the hell does he think he's doing?" Alex muttered under his breath.

Carole glanced at him in surprise. He was clenching the iced tea bottle so hard she was afraid it might shatter. "What do you mean?" she said. "That's just Gary. He and Lisa have a couple of classes together, I think."

Alex took half a step forward, then turned to stare at Carole. "Who?"

"Gary Korman," Carole explained, feeling a little uncomfortable. "Just a guy she knows. No big deal."

What am I doing? she wondered frantically. *I shouldn't interfere. I should just let Alex go over*

81

there—then he'd realize there's nothing to worry about.

Still, she couldn't seem to stop her mouth from babbling on. "Actually, I think one of the classes they have together is physics. They may even have been lab partners last month. I think they were, anyway. Although now that I think about it, I'm not really a hundred percent sure about that. . . ."

"Lab partners, huh?" Alex still sounded suspicious. "If you ask me, he's not acting like he just wants to be lab partners."

Carole wished more than ever that she were somewhere else. She was the last person who should be involved in someone else's relationship. What did she know about jealous boyfriends? Especially one who got all worked up for no apparent reason . . .

"Hey, relax," she joked nervously. "Just because a movie star is in love with your girlfriend, that doesn't mean every guy in the world wants to steal her away from you."

Alex stopped short. Slowly he turned to face Carole again, his face pale. "What did you just say?"

Carole giggled nervously, feeling more uncomfortable than ever. Maybe that hadn't been the most tactful joke in the world—Alex was probably still sensitive about the whole topic. But once again, her mouth seemed to have become detached from her brain as she hastened to explain herself. "N-Never mind," she stammered. "Um, I just meant, you know, the thing with Skye—how he told Lisa over the summer that he liked her as more than a friend . . . You know."

"No." Alex's voice had gone as cold as ice. He turned away from Carole to stare grimly at Lisa. "As a matter of fact, I didn't know. Thanks for letting me in on the secret."

FIVE

Callie watched as A.J. and Julianna tangoed enthusiastically past, clearly oblivious to the beat of the music blasting from the CD player near the fireplace, which bore no resemblance to their own private beat. She shook her head in amusement. "They're really something, aren't they?" she commented to Emily, who was perched on the sofa arm beside her.

"I'll say." Emily paused and took a swig of her ginger ale as half a dozen guys stampeded loudly past, chasing a giggling girl who was carrying a huge bowl of cheese curls clutched to her chest. When they had passed, Emily spoke again. "It's good to see that the real A.J. is back."

"I guess." Callie wasn't so sure that was entirely true—she'd noticed that A.J. was still pointedly ignoring Phil, who was dancing with Stevie nearby—but she didn't want to ruin Emily's good mood. "So how did things go today at Free Rein? I never asked you."

"Great." Emily smiled, but her eyes were a bit wistful. "They were so excited to have PC back. And I know Max would call me crazy, but I'd swear that PC was happy to be back at his old home."

Callie smiled understandingly. Emily had decided to donate her horse, PC, back to the therapeutic riding center where she'd gotten him. That way another disabled rider might be able to discover the joys of riding, thanks to his specialized training. Emily was planning to get a new horse once she got to Australia, and maybe even help train it herself.

Still, Callie knew it must have been hard for Emily to say good-bye to the horse she'd ridden for so many years. She decided it was probably time for a change of subject, before Emily started feeling too sad to enjoy herself.

"Looks like my brother is campaigning his head off," she commented, gesturing to Scott, who was leaning against the wall beside the living room doorway, talking to a small group of people and clearly oblivious to the noise and chaos surrounding him as he waved his hands expressively to illustrate his points. Veronica was right beside him, as she had been all evening so far, smiling broadly at everything he said.

Emily followed her glance. "Stevie should be happy about that." She shifted her gaze to Stevie. "Oops! Then again, maybe not."

Callie turned and saw that Stevie was staring fixedly over Phil's shoulder as they danced, glaring directly at Scott's group. She grinned. "I bet I know why," she told Emily. "She was afraid that Veronica would hang all over Scott tonight and get in his way while he was trying to campaign. Looks like she was right."

Emily giggled. "Leave it to Veronica to ruin Stevie's best-laid plans. That's always been her specialty." She shook her head. "I just hope there's nobody like her over in Australia."

"Don't worry. I think it's safe to say she's one of a kind." Callie's gaze had wandered past Stevie to a solitary figure seated in a chair in the far corner of the room, almost out of sight behind a table full of refreshments. "She's not the only one, either."

"Huh?" Emily glanced toward the corner. "Oh, you mean Ben." She shrugged. "Actually, I was kind of wondering why he bothered to come. He hasn't said a word to me—or to anyone else, as far as I can see."

"It is kind of strange that he'd show up," Callie said thoughtfully. "Especially if he's not going to do anything but sit there and stare into space all night. He doesn't even seem to realize there's a party going on around him." She winced as someone turned up the music another few notches. Raising her voice slightly, she added, "He doesn't look like he's having much fun."

Emily shrugged. "He's always been hard to figure." Her face brightened. "Hey, maybe he's a spy! He's been sent undercover to check up on us, report back to the government—or our parents—about any illicit activities. . . ."

Callie snorted, though she couldn't help smiling at Emily's enthusiastic and creative theory. "If so, he has the world's worst disguise," she pointed out. "He sticks out like a sore thumb." She pursed her lips thoughtfully as an idea occurred to her. "No, I think there's only one possible reason he'd come tonight. He must be interested in someone who's here."

"Interested?" Emily suddenly looked very interested herself. "You mean, like, *interested* interested? Ben?"

"I know, it's a pretty wild idea, knowing him," Callie commented. "He's so antisocial, it's hard to believe he'd ever voluntarily spend time with anyone who didn't have four legs and a mane and eat oats." She shrugged. "But what other explanation is there?"

"You have a point," Emily agreed. "But who—" She broke off with a gasp. "Oh! I know. It's probably *you*!"

"What?"

Emily looked excited. "It makes perfect sense," she argued. "You're beautiful, you're smart, you're horsey—what more could someone like Ben want in a woman?"

Callie laughed uncomfortably. "I don't think so," she mumbled. "If anyone at this party is interested in me—well, anyway, I just don't think that's it."

"Are you sure?" Emily peered at her curiously. "Callie, what is it? You look weird."

"It's nothing." Callie wished she'd never started this line of conversation. The last thing she felt like discussing was her suspicions about a certain guy—a guy who was nothing at all like Ben Marlow except for the fact that Callie wasn't the least bit interested in dating him. A guy who'd been following her around like an adoring puppy since arriving at the party . . .

"Callie?" Emily nudged her with one shoulder. "Come on. Are you sure Ben doesn't like you?"

"I'm sure."

"Then what? What's on your mind?" Emily smiled beseechingly. "Come on, this could be your last chance for a long time to tell me your secrets in person."

Callie sighed. What difference did it make if she told Emily her suspicions? She could use a sensible second opinion to let her know if she was imagining things. And Emily wasn't the type to make fun of her or think she was being conceited. Besides, as she'd said, she was moving halfway around the world in three days. . . . "Well, okay." Callie relented at last. "Actually, it's George. I'm afraid he might—well, I think he might, you know, like me."

"George? You mean George Wheeler? Really?" Emily's eyes widened, and she glanced around the room, clearly looking for George.

"Don't look!" Callie said urgently, grabbing her arm. "He's over by the front window. But don't look now. I don't want him to decide to come over here."

"Too late," Emily said, glancing toward the window. "Here he c—"

She broke off as Carole went barreling past them, almost tripping over Emily's crutches, which were leaning against the front of the sofa. Carole's face was red, and she looked upset.

"Whoa," Callie said, staring after her and doing her best to ignore the fact that she could see George approaching out of the corner of her eye. "What's with her?"

Carole hadn't even noticed her friends as she passed them. She stopped just beyond the sofa and leaned on a side table for support, too busy staring at the scene unfolding in the middle of the room to notice anything else.

Her heart in her throat, she watched as Alex stomped over to Lisa, grabbed her by the arm, and pulled her away from Gary. *What's going on here?* Carole wondered desperately as Alex said something to Lisa, still clutching her by the arm. The music was too loud for Carole to hear his words, but his angry expression was unmistakable. *What did I miss? I would have sworn Lisa told me Alex knew all about what Skye said. Didn't she?*

She searched her memory, trying to dredge up the conversation she and Lisa had had on the trail just three days earlier. Her memory for certain things—things that didn't have to do with Samson, Starlight, her job at Pine Hollow, the cell phone number for Judy Barker, or anything else horse-related—might not always be perfect, but she couldn't believe she could have totally misremembered what Lisa had told her. As she ran back over it in her mind, she felt more certain than ever that she was right. *That situation has caused some tension since I've been back,* Lisa had said. *You know, with Alex . . .*

Regardless of what she thought, though, Alex certainly seemed to be upset about something. He and Lisa were involved in some kind of argument, though Carole couldn't hear a single word.

"Oh, hi, Carole," Stevie said, wandering past and poking Carole in the arm. "Did you get a load of the Snob Queen?"

"Huh?" Carole glanced at Stevie, then quickly returned her gaze to Alex and Lisa, who were glaring at each other as a crowd started to gather around them.

"Veronica," Stevie said, more loudly this time. "Did you see the way she's been hanging on Scott all night?" She waved an arm toward the living room entrance, almost knocking over a petite Cross County girl who happened to be walking by with two cups of fruit punch. "She's totally monopolizing him, and if she doesn't stop it, he'll never be able to . . ." Her voice trailed off, and she poked Carole again. "Hey! Are you listening to me?"

"What? Um, sorry." Carole gulped. "I'm, uh, a little distracted right now."

"Why?" Stevie followed her gaze to Lisa and Alex, and her eyes narrowed. "Hey, what's going on over there?" She took a step forward as if to hurry over and see, but Carole grabbed her sleeve and dragged her back.

"Wait," Carole said, pulling her to a relatively quiet corner beside a bookshelf. "I—I don't quite know what happened. But I think it may be my fault."

"What do you mean?"

Stevie listened without interrupting as Carole described her conversation with Alex, her eyes widening as she heard Skye's name and her jaw dropping as Carole related what the young actor had said to Lisa. Carole felt a little guilty about telling her that part, but since the entire party would probably know all about it soon enough, she figured it didn't matter.

". . . and so then he rushed over there and started yelling," Carole finished helplessly, indicating the couple in the middle of the room, who were almost hidden now by the people surrounding them. "I don't know why."

"*I* know why." Stevie looked horrified. "Alex didn't know any of that stuff about Skye."

"Are you sure?" Carole knew it was a foolish question as soon as she asked it. Stevie and Alex were twins—they might not tell each other everything, but they never kept the important stuff secret for long. If Alex had known about Skye's confession, Stevie would have known by now, too. And it was perfectly obvious to Carole that she hadn't.

Stevie shook her head grimly, glancing toward her brother as the crowd shifted again, revealing him to her. "Wow. It's like his worst nightmare came true."

"Not really," Carole protested. "I mean, it's not like Lisa and Skye actually . . ." She let her voice trail off as she realized the enormity of her mistake. "Oh my gosh. I'm such an idiot. This is all my fault!"

Stevie didn't answer except to shrug, which made Carole feel worse than ever. But just then the CD that had been playing came to an end, inflicting a long moment of relative silence over the crowded room. That was when Carole and Stevie could finally hear what Lisa and Alex were saying to each other—or rather, shouting at each other.

". . . and if you can't trust me, I don't know why we're even bothering!" Lisa was screaming.

Alex's face was red and he was swaying slightly from side to side as he faced his girlfriend, like a cobra waiting to strike. "Trust you?" he hollered back, not even seeming to notice that the music had stopped. His voice was echoing through the room, and all eyes were on him. "What a joke. Why should I trust someone who sneaks around behind my back and lies to my face? It's a good thing Carole told me or I might never have known you were scamming me."

Carole winced. *This can't be happening,* she thought desperately. *It's too horrible. If I could have one wish right now, I'd go back in time and make sure I kept my big fat mouth shut for a change. . . .*

"Oh, really?" Lisa snapped back, her hands on her hips. "Well, if that's the way you feel, maybe we should just forget it. End this whole thing."

"Fine by me," Alex returned hotly. "I wish we'd never even started it!"

Lisa glared at him for a long breathless second. Alex glared back. Nobody in the room made a sound—not Carole or Stevie, not Callie or Emily or George, not Scott or the people in his group, not the dozens of other friends gathered in the Lakes' red-white-and-blue–bedecked living room. Then the CD player clicked on to the next disc and the opening beats of a rap hit throbbed out over the room.

That broke the momentary spell, and Lisa spun on her heel and stormed off toward the hall, pushing past anyone who happened to be standing in her way. Halfway there, her eyes met Carole's. Carole gulped when she saw the fury on her friend's face deepen. When Lisa changed direction and headed toward her, Carole felt her heart start to pound. She glanced at Stevie for help, but Stevie was busy watching Alex, who was stomping off in the opposite direction from Lisa. His face crimson and furious, he kicked viciously at an overstuffed chair, then ran both hands through his hair. Apparently noticing that people were staring at him, he glared around the room and then hurried toward the living room door himself, disappearing up the stairs just outside.

"Uh-oh," Stevie said.

Carole was inclined to agree with that sentiment, especially since Lisa had just about reached them. Carole gulped again and tried to gather her skittering, panicky thoughts for an apology as Stevie took off in the direction her brother had gone in.

Lisa stopped in front of Carole, breathing hard, both hands clenched into tight fists at her sides. Carole opened her mouth. *I'm sorry, I'm so, so sorry, so very sorry, so sorry . . .* , she wanted to cry out to her friend.

But Lisa never gave her a chance to say a word. "I can't believe you did this to me!" she shrieked. "Were you actually trying to ruin my life, or was it just some kind of stupid, idiotic mistake?"

Carole was glad the music had started again, keeping most of the partyers from overhearing. She only wished she didn't have to hear it, either.

"Never mind," Lisa went on bitterly before Carole could say a word. "I don't even care. It doesn't matter. All I know is that this is all your fault. Alex and I are through. I hope you're happy."

That was too much for Carole to take. She wanted to explain, to apologize, to defend herself—it wasn't her fault, how could it be?—but suddenly she knew that it was no use, she just couldn't find the words right then. Lisa's onslaught, her hurtful words, rolled over Carole and overcame her, crumbling all her strength, setting her roiled and guilty emotions free to bubble over. She couldn't handle this confrontation right then, not when she felt like this. . . .

Bursting into tears, Carole pushed past Lisa and ran blindly from the room.

SIX

Stevie knocked on her brother's bedroom door. "Alex?" she called, testing the knob. The door was locked. "Alex, it's me. Let me in."

"Go away," said Alex's muffled voice from the other side of the door.

Stevie wasn't giving up that easily. She didn't think her brother should be alone at a time like this, and she certainly didn't think that he and Lisa should just let things end as they were. She had to get in there to talk to him, help him figure out what to do. "Let me in!" she insisted, rattling the knob again. "Come on. Open the door."

After a moment he relented, opening the door a few inches and peering suspiciously through the crack. "Is it just you?"

"Just me, myself, and I. Now let us all in." Stevie pushed the door all the way open and entered, glancing at her brother's haggard, blotchy face. Inside, the noise of the party faded to a dull, distant roar. "That was quite a scene down there," she said carefully. "Are you okay?"

"What do you think?" Alex closed and locked the door, then wandered aimlessly around his messy room for a moment, finally dropping onto his desk chair with a sigh.

Stevie perched on the edge of the bed, not knowing what to say. She was rarely at a loss for words, but this was a situation she'd hoped never to face. Besides that, her mind was still reeling at what Carole had just told her. She'd known that Skye and Lisa had always been close, but she'd never even suspected that they might—but there was no time to think about that just then. "So . . . ," she said leadingly. "Pretty big shock, huh?"

"Duh," Alex said bitterly, scratching at some chipped paint on the arm of his chair and avoiding Stevie's eyes. "I can't believe she did this to me."

That makes two of us, Stevie thought, but she didn't say it out loud. She was there to try to help her brother through this crisis, not worry about her own relationship with Lisa. "Well, look on the bright side," she said, reaching for irony. "At least this makes her big confession about wanting to maybe stay in California seem pretty minor in comparison, huh?"

"What?" Alex looked up quickly. "What are you talking about?"

"You mean she didn't tell you?" Stevie gulped, annoyed. *She promised,* she thought. *She promised me weeks ago that she'd tell him about that. She knew how I felt about keeping secrets from my own twin!*

"Tell me," Alex ordered.

Even if she could have taken back her words, she wouldn't have done it. Maybe this wasn't the ideal time, but Alex needed to know the truth. And if Lisa hadn't told him, Stevie was going to have to do it. "Okay, now remember I'm just the messenger, okay?" she said. "Just before she came back here at the end of the summer, Lisa got the idea that maybe she should stay on in California. Spend her senior year there, live with her dad and Evelyn, maybe continue with her job on the TV set. She thought it would, like, help expand her horizons more or something like that, I guess. You know how she gets about stuff like that sometimes." She shrugged. "Obviously, she decided to come back here after all. But I guess she really stewed over it for a while."

"She never told me that." Alex's voice was low and nearly emotionless. "I had no idea."

Stevie leaned toward him, examining his face closely. "You're not mad because I didn't tell you about this before, are you?" she asked anxiously. "I mean, I would have, but Lisa promised that she'd—"

"It's okay." Alex cut her off with a weary wave of his hand. "Whatever. I wish you'd told me sooner. But it's okay. It's not like it's even that big a deal compared with . . . that other thing." He shrugged. "It's just like the icing on the cake, you know?"

"What do you mean?" Stevie asked cautiously.

Alex shrugged, a shadow of pain flickering across his angry face. "It proves I can't trust her—not about the big stuff, or even the little stuff. So what's the point?" He scowled. "For all I care, she can rush back to California right now and start dating Skye. Or maybe I should say dating him *again*—who knows what else she hasn't told me about?" He shook his head. "We are so over it's not even funny."

Stevie certainly didn't feel like laughing. "Well, okay," she said helplessly. Once again, she didn't know what to say. She certainly wasn't about to defend what Lisa had done. She was sure that Lisa hadn't actually cheated on Alex that summer—well, 99.9 percent sure, anyway—

but that was hardly the point. Their relationship had always been built on honesty, and now . . .

Stevie took a deep breath. So far she wasn't being much help to Alex. She certainly wasn't making him feel any better. Maybe she shouldn't even try. He didn't have much to be cheerful about at the moment. The only one who could fix this situation, if anyone could, was Lisa herself. And there was no chance of that while Alex was locked up in his room.

"Come on," Stevie said, standing and walking toward her brother. "You can't hide in here all night."

"Why not?" he asked sullenly.

Stevie shoved at him, trying to push him off his chair onto his feet. "Because," she replied firmly, "you can't let her see how much this is bothering you. Right? So buck up and get back out there."

Alex reluctantly stood. "I guess."

"That's the spirit." Stevie hid her smile of satisfaction. Now maybe they were getting somewhere. She couldn't remember how many times she and Phil had stormed off after some stupid argument or other, then made up as soon as they set eyes on each other again, remembering how much they loved each other and how little anything else mattered when you got right down to it. Surely the same thing would happen here. Wouldn't it?

It has to, Stevie told herself as she followed her brother out of the bedroom. *It just has to. . . .*

A few minutes later Callie was standing in the hallway in front of a small table full of food, spreading soft cheese on a cracker, when Alex appeared at her side. "Hi," she said, a little surprised to see him so soon after his knock-down-drag-out, very public breakup with Lisa. Not certain what to say to someone in such a situation, Callie held out her cracker. "Want one?"

"Thanks." Alex accepted the cracker and stuffed it into his mouth. "I'm starved. Stevie barely let us stop for lunch while we were setting up for this party earlier. And as for dinner, forget it." He laughed briefly.

Callie smiled along, wondering what his behavior meant. *Did he and Lisa make up already?* she wondered. But looking at his closed-off and wary expression, she somehow didn't think so. *Maybe he just wants to take his mind off it all. He could probably use some help. I wish Scott were here. He's so good at this sort of stuff. . . .*

She glanced through the living room doorway to where her brother was holding court in the center of another group of eager voters. As usual,

Veronica was glued to his side, smiling proudly as he talked. Her brother, her father, her mother—they were all so good at talking to people, making them feel comfortable no matter what the situation. Callie had often wondered how she had managed to be born without that particular talent.

But there was no time to worry about that now. She could either make an excuse and ditch Alex immediately, or she could do her best to help. After quickly fixing herself another cracker, Callie turned back to Alex with a smile. "So," she said brightly. "Look at Emily over there. She's really having a great time, I think."

Alex glanced at Emily, who was perched on the stairs a few yards away, talking animatedly to a large group of friends. "That's great," he said. "I can hardly believe she's moving so soon."

"I know," Callie agreed. "I'm really going to miss her. She's been an incredible help with my therapeutic riding. Still, I think she'll do great in Australia."

"Definitely. Knowing Emily, she'll be bronco-busting kangaroos before you know it." Alex smiled briefly, his expression lightening slightly.

Callie took that as encouragement that she was helping to improve his mood. "All I can say is it's a good thing she doesn't go to Fenton

Hall," she joked. "If she did, there's no way Scott and Stevie would let her move before that election. And if they did let her, they'd be looking into absentee voting! They're taking their campaign pretty seriously."

"You're right about that. Check it out." This time Alex actually chuckled. He nodded toward Scott's group.

Callie turned and saw that Stevie had just barged in on the group, knocking Veronica aside and planting herself next to Scott. Callie grinned. "Hey, maybe after this election is over, Stevie could get a job with Dad," she commented. "He could use her help chasing away some of the more annoying reporters that are always following him around."

"Sounds good," Alex agreed. "I always knew that Stevie's unique personality must have some useful purpose."

Callie felt proud of herself as she observed his bemused expression. There was still a shadow—sadness, anger, or maybe both—on his face. But he definitely looked more relaxed than he had when he'd first come over to her. Maybe she actually had inherited some of her parents' people skills after all.

"How's it going, A.J.?" Alex said, snapping Callie out of her own self-satisfied thoughts.

Looking up, she saw that A.J. was hurrying toward them. His face was flushed and sweaty under his reddish brown hair, and he looked weary.

He blinked at Alex and Callie as he stopped in front of the food table. "Oh, hi," he said distractedly before grabbing a large handful of crackers and stuffing them into his mouth. "I'm starved," he mumbled through a mouthful of crumbs.

Callie was feeling so pumped up by her success with Alex that she decided to give it another try. She'd noticed that A.J. had been trying really hard all evening to seem like he was having the time of his life, but it was obvious to anyone with two eyes in their head that it was all an act. She guessed that he was still too upset about his adoption to think about much else, even in the middle of a party.

"Listen, A.J.," she said gently as he reached for another handful of crackers. "I just wanted to tell you. We don't really know each other that well or anything, but if you ever need someone to talk to about the whole adoption thing, I'm here for you, okay?"

A.J. stopped short with his hand halfway to his mouth. He stared at Callie. "Oh, really?" he snapped, his voice bitter and harsh. "Great.

Didn't anyone ever think that I might be sick of talking about that? That it's not the only thing I know how to talk about?"

He turned and rushed toward the front door before Callie or Alex could react.

Callie felt like kicking herself. So much for her sudden great understanding of human nature. Why couldn't she just have minded her own business as usual? She knew A.J. couldn't just leave, since Phil had driven him there, but she didn't want him to hide outside by himself and sulk.

She watched anxiously as his girlfriend cut him off before he reached the door. Julianna's pretty face was distraught, and she held out her arms to him beseechingly. A.J. only spun around and raced back down the hall in the opposite direction. His face was grim as he passed Callie and Alex. He veered to the right and disappeared into the narrow hallway leading to the laundry room.

SEVEN

Lisa was locked in the first-floor powder room, trying to get her emotions back under control. It had been a good fifteen or twenty minutes since she and Alex had broken up in front of practically everyone they knew, and she still couldn't quite believe it had really happened.

Why? she wondered as she dabbed at her dripping mascara with a piece of toilet paper. *Why did this have to happen to us?*

She knew at least part of the answer to that—she had kept secrets from Alex, and now she was paying the price. Still, she couldn't help thinking that the price was much too high. Hadn't she kept the secret about Skye precisely because she had known that he might react—or, rather, *over-react*—this way? What else could she have done?

She felt a flush of intense anger as she thought about the way Alex had jumped to conclusions, flown off the handle, acted like a total jerk in

107

front of everyone. But her fury passed as quickly as it had come. Tossing the bit of tissue into the wastebasket under the sink, she sank onto the toilet lid and buried her face in her hands. She wasn't ready to forgive Alex for the way he had acted out there, but the overwhelming finality of what they'd said to each other was just starting to sink in. Could it really be true? Could their relationship—the romance that Lisa had been so sure was the love of her life—truly be over?

I can't believe it, she thought desolately. *It hardly seems possible that my whole life could change just like that, almost in the blink of an eye. That the two of us could just stop caring for each other. Forever.*

The more she thought about it, the more depressed she was. Her feelings were still too raw for her to know quite how she felt about Alex now, but she found herself already mourning the life they'd shared, all the stupid little things she'd taken for granted until she'd realized she'd lost them. Sharing sundaes after school. Tickle fights on the sofa. Stolen underwater kisses in the Lakes' backyard pool. Foot rubs after a long trail ride in tight boots. Always knowing she had the perfect date for every school dance, every Saturday night . . . Even her Thanksgiving plans were ruined now.

Not to mention my friendship with Stevie, she thought, more upset than ever when that occurred to her. She shook her head, feeling as though she might never be able to handle it all.

There was only one thing she knew for sure. If Carole hadn't opened her big mouth, this wouldn't have been happening. Lisa rubbed her eyes angrily as the tears started to come again. How could one of her best friends have betrayed her this way?

Carole was feeling sad and angry herself at that moment. She was sitting on the cold cement floor of the garage, hidden away between the spare refrigerator and the lawn mower, wiping away a few final tears. She had been sobbing her eyes out ever since Lisa had yelled at her, until finally she couldn't cry anymore.

That didn't mean she felt much better, though. She was tempted to stay right where she was for the foreseeable future, hiding and avoiding the consequences of her own thoughtless words. How could one little comment, one secret, have sparked such a huge disaster? She had no idea, and she didn't really want to think about it. She just wanted it all to go away.

She was startled out of her thoughts when the garage door suddenly flew open with a bang and then slammed shut again. A.J. rushed in, his face flushed, but he stopped short when he saw her sitting there.

"Oh," he said flatly. "I didn't know anyone was here." He turned as if to go but then hesitated. "What are you doing out here, anyway?"

"Hiding," she admitted. "Didn't you see what happened in there before?" She brushed at a damp spot on her left cheek and blinked at him.

"Oh. Right," he said as if a lightbulb had just gone on in his head. "Well, okay then." He shot her a cautious glance. "So you're probably not going to start in on me with some sensible discussion of the psychological ramifications of adoption, huh?"

Carole shook her head and sniffled loudly. "I don't think so."

"Cool." A.J. lowered himself to the floor, squatting a few feet in front of her with his arms on his knees. He gazed at her somberly. "So can I hide out here with you?"

Carole gave him a tiny smile, suddenly glad for the company. "Sure. As long as you don't start lecturing me about how I should think before I speak."

A.J. shook his head vigorously. "No way," he

declared. "I'm a big believer in blurting. I try never to think before I speak. When I accidentally do, I just ignore my brain and blurt out whatever I was going to say anyway."

Carole giggled. For once the old A.J. seemed to be back, silly and likable as ever, and she was happy about that. She scooted forward a little, out from the shadow of her hiding place. "Okay, then," she said. "We know what we *don't* want to talk about. So what do you want to talk about instead?"

"How about how thirsty I am? I just ate about a thousand dry, salty crackers, and I'm totally parched." A.J. clutched at his throat and pretended to gag by way of illustration. Then he glanced at the refrigerator beside Carole. "D'you think they stashed any sodas in there?"

"Um . . ." Carole's mind flashed back to the beer she and Alex had found. But before she could respond, A.J. had opened the refrigerator door.

His eyes widened. "Yow," he commented. "Not just sodas."

He shrugged and reached toward the lower shelf, tossing Carole a cola and then reaching for another.

He hesitated. "You know," he said slowly, "who needs soda anyway?" He snapped a can of beer out of its plastic six-pack ring and held it up. "This might be just what the doctor ordered." Before Carole could react, he popped open the top and took a gulp, grimacing for a second but then smiling broadly. "Aaah! Nothing like a nice cold one when you're feeling down."

Carole watched with a feeling of dread in the pit of her stomach, not knowing what to do or say. She felt as if she'd suddenly been dropped into the middle of some horrible made-for-TV movie and she didn't know her next line.

A.J. suddenly seemed to remember her. "Oh, sorry." He grabbed another can and tossed it to her. "Here you go. Bottoms up."

Carole caught the can, almost dropping her soda in the process. She stared at the beer for a long moment, hardly noticing as the icy condensation melted off its smooth surface and dripped down her arm.

Beside her, A.J. had closed the refrigerator and taken another long swig of his beer, sighing with pleasure and wiping his mouth with the back of his hand. Carole continued to stare at her own can, the letters and swirls of the familiar logo burning into her brain. She had never so much as tasted beer before, not in her whole life. But now she wondered what it would be like. It was right there in her hand—it would be so easy. . . .

Maybe A.J.'s right, she thought uncertainly, running her fingers over the pop top, playing with the edge of it. *Maybe a few sips would make me feel better. Put things in perspective.*

She shuddered, the temptation passing as quickly as it had come. Opening the refrigerator door, she shoved the can back inside as if it were a hot potato. "Come on, A.J.," she said urgently, holding the door open as if he might actually return his own half-empty beer. "You know we shouldn't be doing this. Why don't we go back inside now?"

He shrugged and took another swig. "You go ahead if you want. I think I'll stay out here." Reaching past her, he grabbed the remainder of the broken six-pack and tucked it under his arm. "Actually, I think I'm going out for a little fresh air."

Without another word, he headed out the side door of the garage into the Lakes' darkened yard, whistling under his breath. All Carole could do was watch helplessly, still holding on to the open refrigerator door.

EIGHT

After the sixth time someone banged on the door, begging to use the toilet, Lisa gave up and came out. She had touched up her makeup as best she could—she had no idea where she'd left her purse—and she was satisfied that she looked relatively normal.

She didn't feel normal, though. As she emerged from the bathroom, barely avoiding being run down by a grateful Fenton Hall sophomore, she glanced around cautiously. The hall was crowded, but she didn't see many people she knew. She picked her way toward the living room door, awaiting and dreading the moment she would spot Alex.

Pausing in the doorway, she swept the living room with her eyes. There were so many people packed in there that Lisa was surprised it didn't simply burst at the seams. Just inside the doorway, Scott and Veronica were chatting with sev-

114

eral of Veronica's friends. Over on the sofa, Stevie and several of her Fenton Hall school-mates were talking intently with their heads close together, shooting occasional glances at Scott. In the far corner of the room, Ben Marlow was slouched deep into an upholstered chair, looking bored and hostile. On the dance floor, Phil was fast-dancing with Julianna, who kept glancing worriedly toward the doorway, obviously watch-ing for A.J.

Then Lisa spotted Alex. He was over near the front windows, leaning against the wall and chat-ting with Emily as they both chomped on carrot sticks from the bowl Emily was holding. His back was to Lisa, so he couldn't see her standing there, and Emily hadn't noticed her yet, either. Lisa stared at Alex's back, running her eyes over the familiar set of shoulders as she wondered what to do. She was still angry about what had happened, but thinking about what her life would be like without Alex. She couldn't let things stay the way they were.

But how could she fix this? Should she go over, talk to him, try to work it out somehow? Could she bring herself to apologize, even if she didn't really think she'd done anything that wrong? Or should she wait and see whether he came looking for her?

She took a couple of hesitant steps into the room, still not certain of her next move. Before she could decide, she felt a hand on her arm.

"Lisa," Veronica diAngelo purred. "There you are. We were just wondering if you'd disappeared for good."

Lisa turned, gritting her teeth at the unwelcome interruption. She found Veronica staring at her, her expertly lined eyes glittering with frank curiosity. Scott was beside her, holding a pair of soda cups.

"Here I am," Lisa responded as lightly as she could. "Now if you'll excuse me—"

"Wait." Veronica gripped her arm more tightly, her mouth curving into a sympathetic smile. She didn't bother to raise her voice above its normal tone, but Lisa had no trouble hearing every word she said, even over the noise of the party. "Don't run off just yet. Scott and I wanted you to know that if there's anything we can do, or if you need a shoulder to cry on after what happened, we're here for you."

What a joke, Lisa thought. *Veronica's motives are so transparent that a two-year-old could see through them. She's obviously just hoping for some juicy gossip.* She glanced at Scott, who looked uncomfortable. *I guess Scott realizes that, too.*

"Thanks," she said aloud. "But I'm fine."

"Lisa, Lisa." Veronica pushed back her sleek dark hair and leaned closer. "Really. We've all been there, you know. You don't have to hide your—"

"Gary!" Scott boomed out suddenly, setting his sodas on a handy end table and reaching out to grab Gary Korman, who had just wandered into the room. "My man! How's it going? And George Wheeler—I've barely seen you all night. Come on over here and say hello." He gestured to George, who was picking at a bowl of chips nearby.

Despite her state of mind, Lisa smiled. Scott was being almost as transparent as Veronica. It was clear that he hadn't been happy about being drawn into Veronica's prying, and he wasn't wasting any time in doing something about it. Lisa, for one, was grateful. Veronica scowled and stalked off, muttering something about powdering her nose, as Scott started chattering at George about the Colesford Horse Show.

Meanwhile, Gary stepped closer to Lisa and nodded a rather sheepish hello. "Yo," he said. "I was looking for you before. I just wanted to say—" He paused and cleared his throat uncertainly, his droopy eyes blinking. "I wanted to say I'm sorry if, you know, I caused any trouble for you and your boyfriend."

"Of course not," Lisa said in surprise. *Why would he think that?* she wondered.

Gary shrugged and shifted his weight. "Okay," he mumbled. "Because well, you know . . ."

Suddenly Lisa remembered what Alex had said as he'd yanked her away from Gary earlier. *Excuse me,* he'd snapped. *If you're done drooling all over my girlfriend now, I need to talk to her about something.* Lisa had been irritated by his rudeness, but she'd quickly forgotten the comment because of what had happened next. Obviously, though, Gary had been worrying that something he'd done had set Alex off.

"Oh, no, no, no," Lisa hastened to assure him, putting a hand on his arm to emphasize her point and leaning a little closer to make sure he heard her over the blasting music. She smiled at Gary, thinking how good it was to know such a truly nice, concerned guy. "I'm sorry about that. It had nothing to do with you, really. He was just mad about something else, and he took it out on you because you happened to be there."

"Good." Gary looked relieved. "Thanks. I was wondering what I'd done wrong."

Lisa gave his arm one last squeeze before turning to check on Alex again. When she did, she found that he was facing her way. In fact, he was staring straight at her, his face dark and angry.

Her face flamed as, in a flash, she realized what he was thinking. He'd seen her with Gary, watched her leaning toward him as if for an intimate talk, and jumped to the wrong conclusion. Again.

Sure enough, a second later Alex rushed toward the door, his face cold as he passed within a few feet of her. He disappeared into the hall, and a second later Lisa heard the unmistakable sound of the front door slamming.

Carole felt distinctly strange as she wandered through the laundry room and down the narrow back hall, following the sounds of the stereo to the party. In the front hallway, she almost collided with Veronica diAngelo, who shot her a dirty look, which Carole ignored, while she hurried on ahead of Veronica into the living room.

Carole hardly noted the other girl's presence. She was still thinking about the eager look on A.J.'s face as he'd tossed her that beer and the way he'd rushed off with the extra cans. Worrying about what he was up to out there in the dark at the same time she was wondering whether Lisa would ever speak to her again had chased away the last remaining vestiges of her partying mood.

As she entered the living room, Carole immediately spotted Lisa, who was standing just inside the doorway talking to George Wheeler and Gary Korman. They didn't notice her, though, so she scurried past quickly. She knew she would have to face Lisa at some point, but she didn't feel up to it right then. After the scene with A.J., she was feeling too distracted for another argument.

Stevie was nearby, standing with Scott and Veronica and a couple of other Fenton Hall students. They didn't seem to notice Carole's entrance, either. Neither did Phil, who was sitting on the couch with some friends, gulping down cookies and pretzels; or Callie, who was talking to a guy Carole didn't recognize; or Emily, who was just swinging into the room on her crutches, accompanied by a couple of friends.

Am I invisible? Carole thought giddily. *Maybe when I wished I could disappear while Lisa was yelling at me, it actually worked.*

She shook her head, feeling stranger than ever. Suddenly she spotted Ben, who was sprawled in a chair on the far side of the room. She'd hardly seen him since their arrival together, and at the sight of him she felt a rush of relief.

Ben, Carole thought. *He's the one person here who definitely won't care that I'm not in a party mood anymore.*

She hurried toward him. He spotted her when she got close and sat up a little straighter. "Hey," he greeted her.

"Hey," she returned, grabbing an empty chair and pulling it up beside him. She scooted it as close to his chair as possible so that they wouldn't have to shout to make themselves heard over the music. "How's it going?"

Ben shrugged, his dark eyes opaque in the dim light in their corner of the room. "This isn't really my scene."

No kidding, Carole thought, wondering once again why he had bothered to come. "Oh," she said aloud. "Um, I guess it's not really mine, either. I don't go to a whole lot of parties, at least not big ones like this."

"Yeah," Ben said succinctly. He paused for a moment, clearing his throat as he surveyed the busy scene in front of them. "But everyone needs to get away . . . get, um, a change of scene. Hang out with friends."

All at once Carole started to feel awkward. It wasn't like Ben to say so much—while making so little sense. What *was* he trying to say? And why was he staring at her so intently? His expression was impossible to read, and for some reason it was making her palms sweat.

He's never been that friendly with Emily, she thought rather frantically. *So why did he come? Why is he still here? I mean, I'm the only person here he ever talks to at all.* She gulped as the meaning of that last thought struck her full force. *Could it be that . . . Could he . . . Is it possible he might actually . . .*

The wild thoughts popping up in her head were too crazy, too scary and unexpected and strangely intriguing for her to put into words, even in her own mind. Feeling suddenly shy, nervous, and incoherent, Carole wet her lips and did her best to smile at Ben. There was only one way to find out. If only she could work up the nerve. . . .

"So anyway," Ben began after a long pause. "Carole, I . . . I should say someth—"

"Would you—that is, would you like to—" Carole interrupted, her voice coming out a little louder than she'd planned. She swallowed hard and started again. "Um, I mean, would you like to dance?"

Ben stared at her for a long moment, his expression caught between astonishment and confusion. Realizing that a slow, dreamy, ultra-romantic song had just come on the stereo,

Carole felt a hot, prickly blush creeping up her neck to her face.

"I don't dance," Ben said bluntly at last, pushing his chair back and standing up. "I've got to go. It's getting late."

Carole blushed furiously, feeling more humiliated than she'd ever felt in her life, as Ben stalked out of the room without a backward glance.

NINE

Stevie hardly noticed as Ben brushed past her on his way out. She was too busy trying to pry Veronica away from Scott, just as she'd been doing off and on throughout the entire evening.

As if it's not bad enough that she's in my house at all, Stevie thought, gritting her teeth as Veronica blathered on about an upcoming school dance, most likely trying to drop enough hints to convince Scott to ask her. *I've been so busy trying to chase her away from Scott and keep her from ruining his chances in the election that I've hardly even spoken to Emily. Or had enough time to eat any of the food I spent all day putting out. Or seen Phil all night.*

She shot a wistful glance at her boyfriend, who was lounging on the couch with a couple of his buddies from the Cross County basketball team, stuffing his face with junk food. She wished she could be over there with him, hanging out and enjoying herself. But business had to come before pleasure . . . With a sigh, she returned her attention to the problem at hand. She was just about to tactfully suggest that Veronica go and check out the Ping-Pong table in the basement when she spotted Lisa standing nearby, talking to a couple of guys.

Well, well, well. So she's back. Stevie hadn't seen Lisa since the big fight. She glanced around the room in search of her brother, but Alex was nowhere to be seen. She knew that she needed to go and speak to Lisa herself at some point, try to determine where the two of them stood after what had happened. But first she wanted to check in with her brother—if she could find him. *I hope he's not moping around somewhere by himself again,* she thought worriedly, feeling a bit guilty about losing track of him when he was in such a delicate mood.

"Hey, you guys," she said, interrupting Scott in the middle of a sentence. "Listen, I need to find Alex. Do you have any idea where he went?"

Veronica just shrugged. But Sue Berry, one of their classmates who had been standing quietly near the outskirts of the group, glanced toward the hall. "I'm not sure," she said, "but I think he may have gone outside."

"Outside?" Stevie repeated. "Why?" Without

waiting for an answer, she spun around and hurried out into the hall.

A second later she was on the front step, pulling the door shut behind her. As soon as the noise of the party inside was muffled by the door, she heard other sounds coming from the side of the house. The sounds of laughter and voices—familiar voices.

"Alex?" she called, hurrying around the garage into the side yard.

Two faces turned to her guiltily as she rounded the corner of the garage and stopped short in shock. Alex and A.J. had dragged a couple of lounge chairs from the pool shed, setting them up in the grass just outside the garage door. A couple of aluminum cans were balanced on the arm of each chair, gleaming dully in the moonlight spilling over the yard. Each of the guys was holding another can.

"Hey, Stevie," A.J. said.

Alex grinned at her. "Yo, sis. What's up?"

Stevie was too surprised at finding the two of them together to respond for a moment. A.J. and Alex had always gotten along well enough— they were the same age, they both liked sports and cars and action movies, and they were both generally easygoing and likable. But as far as Stevie knew, they'd never spent any time alone together, outside the company of Stevie or Phil or Lisa or their other friends. So finding them hanging out by themselves, especially in the middle of a party, would have been strange enough. But now? The last she'd heard, Alex had been mopey and morose, too busy nursing a broken heart to think about much else. And A.J., despite his best efforts to act normal, was clearly still smarting from the pain of finding out that his parents had never told him the truth about his birth.

You'd never guess any of that by looking at them now, though, Stevie thought. *Relaxing out here, sipping their sodas in the moonlight . . .*

She broke off the thought, doing a double take as she leaned over for a closer look at the cans the guys were holding.

"Hey," she said. "Is that . . . beer?"

A.J. giggled. "Busted!" he sang out.

Alex grinned and raised his can, touching it to A.J.'s before taking a swig.

Stevie put her hands on her hips, shocked. "Are you two crazy?" she blurted out. "What do you think you're doing with that stuff?"

"Chill out, Stevie." Alex sounded a little defensive. "It's not like you caught us with heroin or something. It's just a couple of beers—no big deal. You know I don't usually drink. But after what I've been through tonight . . ." He waved one hand lazily, not bothering to go on.

Stevie sank down onto the edge of A.J.'s lounge chair, not sure what to do. Where had the beer come from, anyway? Her parents rarely drank the stuff, and it wasn't as if anyone at the party was old enough to—

Chad! she thought suddenly. She felt like smacking herself on the head. The answer was so obvious. *He forgot those extra cases he stashed in the garage.* Now that she thought about it, she remembered that Chad and Luke had been kind of rushed on their way out earlier.

But knowing where the beer had come from didn't tell her what to do about it. Glancing at the empty cans on the arms of the chairs, Stevie could see that her brother and A.J. were probably already well on their way to being toasted. If they got a little drunker and decided to move their private party indoors, it wouldn't take long for everyone else to figure out where the beer was coming from. Then things could really get out of control fast.

As if reading her mind, A.J. downed the last gulp of his beer, then stood and stretched. "Whew! It's getting kind of chilly out here. I think I'll grab another brewski and head inside to warm up," he announced.

"Good idea." Alex started to clamber to his feet, almost spilling his can as he caught his foot on the leg of his chair. "I'll come with you."

Stevie gulped, feeling panicky. "Hold it," she commanded, doing her best to keep her voice calm and casual. "What are you, complete wimps? Running inside just because it gets a little nippy?"

It was a stupid challenge, but as Stevie had hoped, the guys were just buzzed enough for it to work. "Who you calling a wimp, little girl?" Alex demanded, puffing out his chest and pounding on it with one fist. "We could stay out here all night if we wanted to. Naked, even. Right, dude?"

"Right." A.J. strutted into the garage and reappeared a moment later with a six-pack balanced on one hand. "I'll drink to that."

"Fine," Stevie said dryly, feeling relieved. "Just do me a favor, okay? Forget the naked part."

"Whatever." Alex reached for one of the beers A.J. had dropped on the end of his chair and popped it open. Then he paused and glanced at Stevie. "Oops, sorry," he said. "Where are my manners? Here." He held the opened beer out to her. "Ladies first."

"No thanks," Stevie said quickly. "I don't feel

like turning into a stumbling idiot just now, thanks."

"Wimp!" A.J. crowed, holding his can aloft. "Stevie's a wimp!"

"Ste-vie's a wimp! Ste-vie's a wimp!" the two guys chanted gleefully.

Stevie rolled her eyes and folded her arms across her chest. "Very funny."

Alex moved toward her and slung one arm over her shoulder. "I don't know, sis," he said. "You're the one who was just ragging on us for wanting to go inside. And now you won't even have a few little sips of beer . . ." He glanced at A.J. "What do you think? If we run, we could beat her inside and then lock her out here to think about what a wimp she is."

"No!" Stevie cried. She couldn't care less about being locked out, but there was no way she could let Alex and A.J. go inside. Not in their condition. Not unless she wanted her perfect party to degenerate into some kind of wild beer bash. "Hold it. I was just kidding." She grabbed the beer out of Alex's hand. "See? I'm no wimp."

A.J. cocked an eyebrow at her. "Oh yeah?" he said. "Then why aren't you drinking yet?"

With a weak grin, Stevie held the beer aloft. "Just waiting for you to make a toast."

"Okay, then." A.J. raised his beer. Alex did likewise. "Here's to . . ." A.J. paused for a moment, scratching his head thoughtfully. Then his eyes lit up. "I know! Here's to the party of the century!"

"Whoo-hoo!" Alex cried before tipping his head back and chugging half his beer.

Stevie raised her can to her lips, too, doing her best not to wrinkle her nose as the first sip of the cold, slightly sour-tasting beer hit her tongue. The guys were watching her, so she kept the can at her lips for a good long time, not wanting to set them off again.

"All right, Stevie!" A.J. raised his can to her in admiration. "Way to chug. Ready for your second?"

"Not quite yet." Stevie took another quick sip. She had no intention of drinking a second beer or even finishing the first. All she had to do was nurse it long enough to keep the guys satisfied—and outside—until she figured out the best way to handle the situation.

Callie glanced over her shoulder as she joined her brother and Veronica. As usual, a small group of admirers was gathered around them, most of whom Callie recognized as friends of Veronica's. But Scott immediately made space beside himself for his sister, smiling a welcome. "Hi," he said. "Having fun?"

"Sure." Callie checked the doorway again. Realizing that Veronica and the others were staring at her curiously, she did her best to compose herself and act normal. "Um, hi, everyone. Wasn't Stevie here just now? I wanted to talk to her about something."

Veronica pursed her lips. "Stevie? I guess she was hanging around here before."

Betsy Cavanaugh, one of Veronica's friends, shrugged and tossed her head. "Yeah. But she ran off a few minutes ago." The others nodded.

"Oh." Callie chewed on her lower lip in frustration. She'd really wanted to talk to Stevie about George. Stevie was good at figuring out what to do in sticky situations, and Callie could use a second opinion about the one she was in with her not-so-secret admirer.

I guess it's probably not a good time to catch her, she thought. *I mean, not only is she in charge of keeping, like, a hundred people under control and not letting her house get destroyed, but on top of it all, her brother just broke up with her best friend.* She glanced around, realizing that she hadn't seen Alex for quite some time, although Lisa was across the room chatting with some people Callie didn't know.

Callie forced herself to tune into the conversation around her, smiling blandly as Veronica droned on and on about Scott's ideas for refurbishing the Fenton Hall cafeteria. Scott sipped at his soda and watched Veronica calmly, not seeming to mind that she kept touching his arm every two seconds and gazing up at him adoringly in between.

Ugh, Callie thought. *How can he stand it? She's so clingy and obvious.*

She shuddered, reminded once again of George. Over the past hour it had become uncomfortably clear that he thought of her as more than a friend. He'd turned up in every room, wriggled into every group she was in. Everywhere she looked, he was there, smiling hopefully at her or offering to bring her a drink. It was driving her crazy.

He's being almost as obvious and relentless as she is, she thought, watching as Veronica threw her head back and laughed too loudly at some comment Scott had just made.

Then Callie started to feel a little guilty about her thoughts. It wasn't really fair of her to compare George to Veronica. After all, Veronica was pushy, self-centered, and obnoxious, while George was really just a perfectly nice, rather naive guy who wanted to get to know her. What was wrong with that? Okay, he wasn't exactly an Adonis, but he was sort of cute in a puppy-dog kind of way. Maybe he deserved a chance?

Callie shook her head, suddenly disgusted with herself. When she thought about it that way, she realized she was no better than Veronica. Maybe that was why she always seemed to end up with the male versions of Veronica—self-absorbed losers who cared more about being seen with her than in learning what made her tick.

Well, now here's a sweet, smart, caring guy who really seems interested in me, not just in my looks or my family, and I'm already writing him off. Why can't I go ahead and give the nice guy a chance? Who knows, it might be good for me.

At that moment she caught a glimpse of George, who was over near the fireplace talking to Emily. He was standing with a cup of punch in one hand and a cookie in the other, his round cheeks slightly pink from the heat of the crowded room, his short, wavy hair a bit rumpled, his corduroy pants a tad too short. Maybe he *wasn't* puppy-dog cute. In fact, he looked just about as dumpy and uncool as he possibly could, and Callie shook her head in dismay, knowing it was no good. She couldn't do it. She would never be able to take him seriously as a guy. Would she?

She was saved from trying to figure out the answer by Julianna, who rushed up to the group, looking anxious. "Hi!" she said breathlessly, cutting off one of Veronica's endless monologues. "Listen, have you guys seen A.J.? He disappeared ages ago, and nobody knows where he is."

TEN

Lisa had spent the past half hour swinging back and forth between feeling sorry for herself and feeling furious at Alex. She still couldn't believe the bad luck that had caused him to look over right when she was leaning toward Gary. After what he'd just learned about her and Skye, it was no wonder he'd jumped to the wrong conclusion.

Then again, as she reminded herself more than once, it still hadn't been fair of him to rush off without giving her a chance to explain. Even if he was feeling wounded about the Skye thing, it shouldn't give him an excuse to throw away more than nine months of good times. Hadn't the trust they'd had in each other during that time meant anything to him in the end? Was he really willing to allow one little incident—one where she hadn't even done anything wrong except neglect to tell him about it—to destroy everything they'd built together?

As those thoughts ran through her head in an endless circle, she wandered aimlessly from one group of people she didn't know very well to another, making mindless small talk, hardly noticing what anyone said to her or what she said back. It was tempting to just leave the party— she certainly wasn't having much fun—but she knew that wasn't really an option. Her mother wasn't expecting her home for a couple of hours at least, and Lisa was afraid to think too hard about what she might interrupt if she went home now.

She drifted away from a gaggle of girls who kept talking about a movie she hadn't seen and found herself on the outskirts of the group huddled around Scott Forester. Veronica was holding court, one hand resting lightly on Scott's arm as she pontificated on all the reasons Fenton Hall needed to hold a school dance soon. Lisa nodded a hello to Callie, who was standing beside her brother looking rather bored and restless. Then she pasted a bland smile on her face and pretended to listen, at the same time letting her eyes roam around the room, checking for Alex. She hadn't seen him since he'd stormed out earlier, and she wondered where he'd gone. After all, this was his house.

Speaking of which, I haven't seen Stevie in a while, either, Lisa thought absently. She couldn't help feeling relieved about that. A little while earlier, she'd noticed Stevie looking at her and had been sure she was going to come over, wanting to talk about what had happened with Alex. But then Stevie had turned away and headed for the hallway instead, and Lisa had let out a sigh of relief. She didn't really want to face Stevie until she figured out how she actually felt about Stevie's twin. She also didn't particularly want to deal with Carole, which was why she was glad that she seemed to have disappeared, too.

Actually, Lisa wasn't even sure she wanted to find Alex, though she couldn't seem to stop watching for him to reappear. What would she say to him? She had recognized the stubborn look he'd had on his face when he'd stormed out of the house. She'd seen that look before, though never directed at her. It meant that his anger and his wounded pride had taken over and his brain had switched off. There was no way he was going to be reasonable about what had happened, at least not until he'd had a chance to cool off. Of course, Lisa wasn't feeling very reasonable herself at the moment. If she got a chance to talk to him, she wasn't sure whether she would burst into tears and beg his forgiveness or scream at him for being such a jerk.

Lisa continued to scan the crowds around her. Everyone seemed to be smiling, dancing, having fun, enjoying themselves. That was only right— it was a party, after all. As she watched a couple of guys clowning around in front of Emily, hopping like kangaroos and making her laugh, Lisa felt a pang of self-pity. This was such a special night for Emily, and it should have been a special night for Lisa and Alex, too. Now it was completely ruined, all because of a stupid misunderstanding. The thought made her so weary that she almost couldn't stand it. What if she and Alex didn't work things out? How many other special occasions would end up being as painful as this one when she was forced to face them alone instead of with him at her side? She and Alex were supposed to go to the Willow Creek High School homecoming dance the next weekend. They had made plans to go to the Colesford Horse Show two weeks after that to cheer on Carole and Stevie and their other friends who were entered. And of course, looming on the horizon just beyond that was Thanksgiving.

So much for all our romantic plans for eating

turkey together, Lisa thought helplessly. *We'll be lucky if we're even speaking by then. I'll probably end up having to pass the cranberry sauce to Rafe after all. . . .*

Suddenly she blinked as she remembered that there was still another option open to her. She hadn't mentioned her plans with Alex to her mother yet. She hadn't even told her father that she wasn't coming to California.

I could still go out there, she realized, her heart starting to pound at the thought. *Why hang around Willow Creek and be miserable when I could be relaxing in sunny California with people who aren't mad at me, like Alex and probably Stevie, or driving me crazy, like Mom and Rafe?*

The more she thought about the idea, the more perfect it seemed. Obviously, dinner at the Lakes' was off now that she and Alex were off. And even if Rafe didn't actually come to her house for Thanksgiving, she didn't want to spend the holiday listening to her mother talk about him.

Getting away from my problems for a little while might just give me some perspective on them, she thought with anticipation, loving her new idea more and more the longer she considered it. *Or at the very least, it will give me a chance to just forget about everything and relax for a few days. I could spend some time with Lily, go to the beach, maybe get Dad and Evelyn to help me with my college applications, see all my friends from the summer. . . .*

"Excuse me," she mumbled to Scott and Callie and the others around her, suddenly unable to wait one more minute to put her new plan into action. She'd spent so much of the evening feeling helpless—but now she was going to take back control of her life. She was going to call her father right now and give him the good news.

She slipped away from the group and headed for the stairs. Moments later she was peeking into Stevie's bedroom, which was dim and empty and relatively quiet, though the noise from the party still seeped up through the floorboards and made the whole house seem to throb as if alive. Closing the door softly behind her, Lisa hurried across the room, perched on the edge of Stevie's bed, and picked up the phone from her bedside table.

Her father had given her a private phone code when he'd first moved to California, which meant she wouldn't have to worry about reimbursing the Lakes for the long-distance call. As she punched in the familiar numbers, Lisa prayed that her father would be home.

"Hello?"

Lisa smiled when she heard his voice. "Hi, Dad. It's me."

"Me who?" he joked, as he'd done since she was a little girl calling him at the office.

"Me, the one who's coming to California for Thanksgiving," she replied.

"Really?" Her father sounded surprised but thrilled. "Are you serious? You're going to come? That's great!"

"I can't wait to see you—all of you."

"We can't wait to see *you*," he answered. "This is such a nice surprise—we were starting to think you weren't going to be able to make it. I know you're awfully busy these days. Speaking of which, aren't you supposed to be at some kind of party right now?"

Lisa gulped and clutched the phone tighter. She didn't feel like explaining the reasons for the timing of her call. "Um, sort of. Oops! I think that was call waiting," she lied. "I'd better go, okay?"

"Sure," her father agreed. "I'll call and let you know once I make the arrangements for your plane ticket. Talk to you then, sweetheart."

"Bye, Dad." As she hung up the phone, an intense feeling of relief washed over her. It was done. Soon she would be able to escape from all the problems that were weighing her down.

Soon, but not soon enough. She only wished that Thanksgiving break started the next day instead of a whole month from then.

Carole slumped deeper into the well-worn upholstered chair, once again feeling invisible. This time she was glad. She had come down into the Lakes' basement rec room specifically to avoid having to talk to anyone. Ever since Ben had stomped out of the party some twenty minutes earlier, she hadn't felt capable of carrying on any sort of conversation.

Fortunately the dozen or so other people in the basement seemed perfectly willing to let her be. The only person who had even glanced at her when she'd crept down the stairs had been Gary Korman. He seemed to be deeply involved in some kind of intense Ping-Pong tournament, though, so he had merely nodded a casual hello from his spot at the table and then apparently forgotten her presence. Carole didn't know any of the other people who were hanging out around the Ping-Pong table, so she had just sat there pretending to watch match after match from her chair in the corner, nursing her injured feelings and worried thoughts in privacy.

She still couldn't believe how much it had hurt when Ben had glared at her and then left her feeling like the world's biggest fool. Carole didn't pretend to be any kind of expert when it came to guys—far from it—but she still couldn't believe she'd made such a huge, humiliating mistake.

How could I have actually believed that Ben came to this party because he liked me? she thought. *How could I have been so conceited, so completely delusional?* As her eyes followed the Ping-Pong ball back and forth, back and forth, she wondered how she would ever be able to face Ben again.

The worst part was, he wasn't the only one she was afraid to face. Lisa had been angry at her, and no wonder—thanks to Carole, her perfect romance with Alex was in ruins. Carole wouldn't be surprised if Lisa never wanted to speak to her again. Even Stevie had looked at her as if it were all her fault.

Carole had thought about just getting up and leaving the party. After what she'd done, she was probably the least welcome person in the world at the Lakes' house. But somehow she couldn't work up the energy. It just seemed too hard to climb out of her comfortable, private chair and go all the way upstairs. For one thing, she would be sure to run into people she knew who might start asking her questions, wanting to talk about what had happened. Worse yet, she might encounter Lisa, or maybe Stevie or Alex. She wasn't sure she could handle seeing any of them without bursting into tears again.

Besides, where would she go if she left? Her first instinct would be to head over to Pine Hollow, find comfort in the familiar sounds and smells of the nighttime stable, spend time with creatures who wouldn't judge her, wouldn't think she was a terrible person. . . . But she couldn't go there now. Not when there was even the slightest chance that Ben might be there.

No, it was safer just to stay where she was. Watching the little white ball bounce back and forth was starting to give her a headache, so Carole closed her eyes for a moment. Even though there were people all around her, she'd never felt so alone in her life.

Her eyes flew open again when she heard heavy footsteps clattering down the creaky wooden staircase. "Yo!" a tall guy with thick, floppy black hair called to the group as he leaned over the banister. Carole couldn't remember the guy's name, but she vaguely recognized him as a friend of Gary's. "Guess what?" the guy continued. "There's beer out in the garage!"

"Beer?" Gary's Ping-Pong opponent looked away, ignoring the ball as it bounced off his arm and dropped beneath the table. "Are you sure, dude?"

"Come see for yourself." The black-haired guy disappeared back up the stairs.

Gary dropped his paddle on the table. "Let's go," he said eagerly. Within seconds, the entire group had stampeded upstairs, leaving Carole completely alone.

Uh-oh, she thought, sitting bolt upright in her chair, suddenly distracted, at least a little, from her own problems. *Someone found Chad's beer. This is bad news.*

Once again she was tempted to leave. She didn't want to be around if things got too wild, and she knew her father would have a fit if he found out she'd been at a party where people were drinking. Still, she knew she couldn't just run away and leave Stevie and Alex alone to deal with this mess. Whatever Stevie might think of her at the moment, Carole's duty as a loyal friend was to stay and help try to keep things under control.

Reluctantly, she dragged herself out of the chair and headed for the steps, her heart in her throat as she heard whoops and shouts from overhead. When she reached the top of the stairs, which opened out into the narrow hall leading to the laundry room and garage, she saw a steady

146

stream of people pushing their way toward the open garage door. A few others were pushing their way back in, each of them holding one or more cans of beer.

Carole gulped and turned the opposite way. She had to find Stevie and let her know what was going on in case she didn't know already. Pushing her way past a couple of guys chugging at the end of the passage, she turned into the front hall and raced toward the living room door.

But she stopped short before she reached it, gasping in shock. "S-Stevie?"

Stevie didn't hear her. She was standing just inside the front door talking to A.J. with a big grin on her face—and an open can of beer in her hand.

ELEVEN

Callie was talking to Emily when she felt someone sling an arm around her shoulder. Startled, she turned to see who it was, half expecting it to be George. She'd managed to avoid him for the past few minutes, slipping away from Scott's group when George had joined it and hiding out in the hall until she'd seen him wander by toward the kitchen. But she had been distracted by her conversation with Emily and wouldn't have noticed if he'd returned.

To her surprise, it was Alex. He was grinning at her, his face mere inches from hers.

"Hey, Callie," he breathed. He squeezed her shoulders tightly. "Want to dance?"

She wrinkled her nose. There was no mistaking the smell of beer on his breath, and she couldn't help feeling shocked. Callie had known a few people back in her old hometown who got wasted at every party they went to, but she wouldn't have expected that sort of thing from her new friends in Willow Creek. They didn't seem like the type.

"Um, not right now, thanks," she told Alex, trying not to let her disgust show in her face or voice. "Maybe later."

"Aw, come on." Alex hadn't removed his arm. "Pretty please?"

Callie glanced at Emily for help, but the other girl's face had paled and she was backing slowly away. It was obvious that she had no idea what to do and couldn't think of anything but escape. Callie sighed, but she couldn't really blame her. She would just have to deal with this problem herself.

"Come on, Callie, what do you say?" Alex persisted, his speech sounding a little slurred. His arm tightened around her even more. He didn't seem to notice as Emily finally turned and fled. "I'll hold you so tight you won't even need those crutches."

Callie wriggled her shoulders. "Let go," she ordered as firmly as she could manage. "You're hurting me."

"Oops." Alex let go of her immediately, smiling sheepishly. "Sorry about that. Come on, let me make it up to you. Dance with me." Leaning closer, he put one finger to his lips and winked conspiratorially. "I probably shouldn't tell you this, but I've always thought you were reery pletty. Oops. I mean, reery *pretty.*"

Wow, he's bombed, Callie realized. *What am I going to do? In his condition, who knows how he'll react if I blow him off? Maybe it would be easier if I just go ahead and—*

"Hi there," a new voice interrupted.

Callie turned and saw George standing beside her. Emily was just behind him, smiling nervously but hopefully. "Hi, George," Callie said, realizing she'd never been so glad to see him in her life.

Alex had turned to glance at the newcomer as well. "Hey," he mumbled. "What's up?"

"Hope you don't mind, Alex," George said with an apologetic smile. "I'm going to have to steal Callie away from you now. She promised me this dance—it's my favorite song."

Callie held her breath. She realized that Emily must have fetched George, hoping to rescue her from Alex that way. Would it work? Or would it just get George a punch in the gut for his trouble?

"Oh," Alex said, a momentary look of confusion crossing his face. He swayed slightly on his feet, then straightened up and nodded. "No problem. Enjoy." He tossed George a mock salute and a wink, then stepped back a few feet, almost crashing into a small side table.

"Shall we?" George moved toward Callie, offering his arm.

She took it gratefully, dropping her crutches against a chair and shooting Emily a quick smile as she followed George to the dance floor, limping slightly despite his help. George turned to face her, taking one hand in his own and resting his other hand lightly on her waist. Callie was a little surprised. The song that was playing, a recent pop hit, was breezy and quick, with plenty of Latin influence. Most of the other couples who were dancing were just fast-dancing the way they would to any up-tempo song, or swaying along and improvising as best they could to the lively beat. But as George swung her around and started moving, Callie quickly realized that he actually knew what he was doing. His feet flashed expertly as he caught the rhythm of the music.

What do you know, Callie thought with amazement. *A guy who can actually dance.*

She had taken endless years of ballroom dancing classes back in her younger days, so she had no trouble keeping up, even with her weak right leg. In fact, she couldn't help noticing that George was being careful to allow for her injury, keeping them in one spot so that she could put most of her weight on her left leg. Meanwhile, his right arm was supporting her firmly as it circled her waist. For once, Callie hardly remembered her disability as she let herself enjoy the dance.

I guess I shouldn't be so surprised, she thought idly as George dipped her expertly. *I mean, he doesn't exactly look like an accomplished salsa dancer. But then again, he doesn't look like he'd be such an incredible rider, either. It just goes to show how stupid it is to judge by appearances.*

She found herself thinking harder about that. Once again, she wondered why she shouldn't at least give George a chance. Maybe the romantic sparks weren't flying for her at the moment, but he was a kind, smart, talented guy. It was stupid to write him off as potential boyfriend material just because he wasn't ready for the cover of *GQ*—stupid and shallow. She should give him a shot. What would be the worst that could happen?

Of course, I shouldn't get ahead of myself here. I don't even know for sure that he likes me as more than a friend, she reminded herself. *For now, I should just relax, stop overanalyzing everything, and enjoy this dance.*

As George bent her into another graceful dip, she did her best to do just that.

A few minutes later Lisa came down the stairs feeling better than she had since the breakup. After finishing her phone call to her father, she had spent a few minutes in the upstairs bathroom, once again trying to salvage what was left of her makeup. Fortunately she had found some of Stevie's supplies in the medicine cabinet and borrowed what she needed, including a comb for her hair, which she was dismayed to find had gotten rather bedraggled over the course of the evening.

She spotted Emily hovering at the bottom of the stairs, staring in the direction of the living room doorway. "Hi," Lisa greeted her. "How's the guest of honor?"

"Worried," Emily said frankly, glancing up as Lisa came down the last few steps.

"What do you mean?" Lisa asked, surprised. "What's going on?"

Emily grimaced. "Didn't you hear?" she asked. "This has turned into some kind of keg party or something." She gestured at a group of guys who were standing in the doorway, laughing and talking loudly. Lisa noticed that most of them were holding beer cans.

She gulped. "Uh-oh," she said. "Does Stevie know about this yet?"

At that moment, Stevie came running out into the hall with a whoop, and Phil was right behind her. Stevie slid on the Oriental rug, almost spilling the beer she was holding as she laughingly fought off Phil's attempts to tickle her.

"My guess is that she knows," Emily replied dryly.

Lisa's heart started beating faster. Apparently a lot had happened in the short time she'd been upstairs. As Stevie and Phil raced off toward the back of the house, Lisa made her way over to the living room entrance and peeked in. The room was as crowded as ever—people were talking, dancing, and laughing. But now a lot of those people were also drinking. Lisa seemed to spy beer cans everywhere she looked.

Emily had followed her. "From what I can tell, A.J. started it. He found some beer out in the garage and helped himself. When other people noticed he was drunk, they made him tell them where he'd gotten it." She shrugged. "Before long, everyone was joining in."

"So I see," Lisa said grimly. She had just spotted Alex. He was on the dance floor, jumping around with A.J. and Julianna. All three of them were holding beer cans. Alex's face was red, and his eyes were glittering strangely as he leaped and spun around energetically with little regard for the actual beat of the music. As Lisa watched, a pretty blond girl in a tight minidress walked past the trio. Lisa recognized her as Nicole Adams, a Fenton Hall student who was a member of Veronica's clique. Alex's eyes lit up when he saw her. He grabbed Nicole by the arm and pulled her to him, making the beer can she was holding fly out of her hand. Neither of them noticed as the can fell and a frothy stain spread over the floor. Alex was too busy pawing at Nicole's hair and planting a big kiss on her cheek as she giggled and pushed him away playfully, not seeming to mind his obnoxious behavior. Disgust bubbled up in Lisa and she had to turn away, feeling almost physically ill. She forced her gaze back to Emily. "But Stevie—"

"I know." Emily blinked. "It doesn't seem like her, does it?"

Lisa shook her head helplessly. Until that moment, she would have said that Stevie Lake was one of the people she knew best in the whole world. But she never would have predicted this. What could Stevie have been thinking?

Just then A.J. broke away from the dancers around him—including Alex and Nicole, who had their arms wrapped around each other by now and were swaying dreamily with their eyes squeezed shut, slow-dancing despite the upbeat tempo of the music.

Lisa couldn't stand to watch. She waited until A.J. reached the doorway, then grabbed him. "Hey, what's wrong with you?" she snapped, some of her anger at Alex coming out in her words.

A.J. didn't seem to notice. He was humming along to the music, slapping his thigh with one hand to the beat. "Huh?" he said, interrupting himself and blinking at Lisa. "Oh, hey. I think Alex was looking for you before." Casting a glance back at the dance floor and spying Alex, who was now running his hands slowly up and down Nicole's back, A.J. let out a high-pitched giggle. "Oops! Maybe not. Now, if you'll excuse me, I'm kind of thirsty. I was just on my way out to the garage to take care of that."

Lisa gritted her teeth. "Listen, A.J., you have to snap out of it."

"Yeah, come on, A.J." Emily's voice sounded desperate. "Quit it with the beer, okay? This wasn't supposed to be that kind of party."

Lisa glanced over and saw that Emily looked more upset than ever. Guessing that all the drinking was starting to scare her, Lisa let go of A.J.'s arm. It was clear they weren't going to get through to him, anyway—he was too far gone. "Listen, Emily," she said as A.J. danced off down the hall. "What do you say we get out of here? I'll drive you home if you want."

Emily accepted gratefully. "Thanks. I was just thinking about calling my parents, but, well, you know. . . ."

Lisa nodded, understanding perfectly why Emily didn't want her parents to witness what was going on, even though she herself hadn't had anything to drink. However idiotic Stevie was acting, neither of them wanted to get her in trouble. And she would definitely be in trouble if her parents ever found out what was going on here—*big* trouble. Lisa could only hope that her mother and Rafe didn't decide to take a romantic moonlight stroll through the neighborhood and stop in to say hi.

"Come on," she told Emily. "Help me find my purse. Then we're out of here."

TWELVE

Carole emerged from the living room and glanced down the hall just in time to see Lisa and Emily disappear out the front door. But she didn't have time to think about that. After spotting Stevie with that beer, she had looked around and found that most of the people she knew were drinking, too—Phil, A.J., Julianna, Alex. Carole had tried to make her way over to Stevie, hoping it wasn't too late to talk some sense into her, but she'd gotten trapped by the crowd and lost sight of her. Now it was all she could do to keep herself from panicking.

As she glanced around for a sensible face in the crowd of partyers all around her, Carole saw Stevie step out of the powder room under the stairs. Carole hurried forward and grabbed her by the arm.

"Stevie!" she exclaimed. "There you are. This

is really bad news. We've got to do something about all this beer."

Stevie grinned and threw her arms around Carole, hugging her tight. "Carole!" she cried joyfully. "I was wondering where you were. I missed you."

"That's nice." Carole pushed her away, forcing herself to be patient. "But listen. You have to stop this. Things are getting out of hand."

"What d'you mean?" Stevie shrugged and leaned against the stairs. "Things are just starting to get fun. Just relax and go with it." Suddenly she smacked herself on the forehead. "Oops! That reminds me. Forgot something." She darted back into the powder room, emerging with a can of beer. She took a long, thirsty drink. "Aaah! That's better," she announced with a burp.

Carole didn't know what to do. She couldn't believe what was happening. Stevie had done plenty of wild and crazy things in her life, but this was different. As far as Carole knew, Stevie had never had more than a few sips of champagne at New Year's in her whole life.

Maybe that's why she's acting so goofy now, Carole realized. *Even if she's only had one or two beers, it would hit her really hard because she has no tolerance for alcohol.*

She still couldn't imagine what would make Stevie drink one or two beers in the first place, but there was no time to worry about that now. Someone needed to take some action, before things got any worse. Obviously, Stevie was in no condition to do it herself, which meant it was up to Carole.

But what can I do? she thought desperately as Stevie wandered off in search of Phil. *I'll never be able to convince everyone to stop drinking. I should probably just call Dad or the police or someone.* She gulped, feeling paralyzed at the thought of what would happen if she did that. Stevie and Alex would be in big trouble with their parents, and if the police got involved, they might even be arrested, for all Carole knew. *Maybe I could call Max instead,* she thought hopefully. *He might agree not to tell anyone. . . .*

She didn't bother to finish the thought, knowing that the stable owner would never agree to that plan. He was just as certain to tell Stevie's parents about the beer as any other adult.

Carole leaned against the staircase and chewed on her lower lip, feeling trapped. She couldn't let things go on this way. All these people had to get home eventually. Suppose the people who were drinking ended up trying to drive? Who knew what could happen then?

Still, she couldn't quite bring herself to go to the phone and call her father. *Everyone would really hate me then,* she thought helplessly. *And I already feel unpopular enough tonight, thanks to the fight with Lisa and then what happened with Ben.*

Before she could make up her mind about what to do, she noticed Alex heading toward her through the crowd. He wasn't holding a beer at the moment, but Carole could tell that he'd had a few already. If Stevie was tipsy, her brother was drunk. As Alex stopped in front of Carole, he seemed unable to stand up straight. He kept swaying and grabbing the staircase for support.

"Carole! Am I glad to see you," Alex cried, his words running together so that it was hard to understand him.

"Um, hi," Carole replied tentatively.

"I want to thank you." Alex swayed dangerously again, and this time he grabbed Carole for balance instead of the stairs, almost knocking her over. "You've saved me a lock—ah, I mean a *lot* of heartache by telling me the truth like you did."

Carole felt incredibly uncomfortable. Trying to ignore the weight of Alex's body pressing on her as he clutched her shoulder for support, she cleared her throat. "Oh. Well, I don't really think—"

"No, seriously," Alex insisted, leaning so close that she could smell the beer on his breath. "I appreciate it. I mean, otherwise I might never have known what Lisa's really like. I never would have known that she's so selfish that she only cares about herself, not me. Only herself."

Carole couldn't help being shocked. Even as drunk as he was, she couldn't believe that Alex would say those things about the girl he loved. He and Lisa had always been such a close, caring couple. . . .

Alex lurched forward again. Fearing he was going to fall, Carole grabbed him by the front of his shirt. He responded by slinging both arms around her. "Lemme give you a hug to say thanks," he murmured, pulling her toward him before she could protest.

Carole wasn't sure how to react, especially when he turned his face toward hers and she suddenly felt his wet lips doing their best to latch on to her own. With a startled shriek, she yanked her head back and struggled against him, pushing him away.

He didn't resist, moving back and leaning against the staircase just as A.J. appeared around the corner from the direction of the garage, several unopened beers in his hands. "Yo," he said, apparently unaware of what he had almost interrupted. "Anyone ready for another?"

"Right here," Alex replied, reaching out to take one of the cans.

Carole couldn't stop shaking as she turned and raced up the hall away from the guys, who seemed unaware of her departure. She hurried into the living room, seeking safety in numbers—and still hoping to find someone sane and sober to talk to, to help her figure out how to clean up this mess. She glanced around, searching for familiar faces, but everyone she saw looked strange and different from the way they usually did. Everywhere she looked, people were chugging down more and more beer. . . . Suddenly she spied Scott Forester near the fireplace, talking to Veronica and some of their schoolmates, and she felt a flash of hope. Maybe Scott could help. He was a natural leader, and he had too much sense to—

She stopped short as she got closer—close enough to see him clearly raise a beer can to his lips and take a sip.

From her position near the front windows, Callie was happy to see that Carole, at least, didn't seem to have succumbed to the urge that had overtaken just about everyone else. Judging by the worried look on her face as she entered the living room, she was just as unimpressed as Callie herself with the way everyone was behaving. George, too, was still sober—Callie could see him sitting on the sofa across the room, looking slightly nervous as he watched the chaos grow around him.

Callie continued to scan the room, noting that Alex and A.J. had just returned from wherever they'd gone. The two of them, together with Stevie, Phil, and Julianna, were playing an impromptu game of crack the whip in the middle of the floor. A.J. stood still as the others formed a chain with him at one end. Then he started spinning around in place, forcing the others to race along faster and faster until they lost their grip on each other's hands and went flying off wildly in all directions, crashing into people and furniture.

I can't believe how stupid a little beer can make some people, Callie thought, shaking her head in disgust. She couldn't imagine what pleasure anyone could possibly get out of such a complete loss of control. *I mean, I guess maybe I can sort of understand why Alex and A.J. would want to drown their sorrows.* She grimaced as she remembered the way Alex had pawed at her as he'd asked her to dance earlier. *But I can't believe that Stevie and Phil would go along with it. Scott either.*

She cast a glance at her brother, who was waving his beer can around as he talked. She pictured how their father would react if news got out that his clean-cut teenage son was drinking at a party. It wasn't exactly the image the congressman was trying to project, and Callie couldn't blame him.

Enough is enough, she thought. *I've got to talk some sense into Scott before it's too late.*

She marched over to the group in front of the fireplace. "Okay, Scott, what's with you?" she demanded, not even caring what Veronica and her hangers-on thought of her. "What do you think you're doing? You know you shouldn't be drinking that."

Veronica tossed her head. "Thank you!" she exclaimed with relief. "That's what I've been trying to tell him for the past ten minutes."

Callie stopped short, staring at Veronica in surprise. It was the last response she would have expected. "Huh?"

"Drinking is really stupid." Veronica crossed her arms over her chest and glared at two or three others in the group who were holding beer cans. "Anybody with any sense at all knows that." She turned her annoyed gaze back to

Scott. "Plus, need I remind you? It's certainly not going to help your chances in the election if word gets out that you're some kind of drunken bozo."

Callie didn't know why, but she'd been sure that Veronica had been the one who'd given Scott that beer. It seemed she'd been completely wrong. "Right," she agreed uncertainly before glancing at Scott again. "So, what's the deal?"

Scott shrugged and laughed agreeably. "Hey, don't jump all over me, you two," he said. "Someone handed it to me, and I took a few sips. That's all."

"Then you won't mind if I just get rid of it for you, right?" Veronica reached over and grabbed the can out of his hand, turned, and unceremoniously dumped the remainder of its contents into a nearby potted plant. Callie winced, imagining what Mrs. Lake would say the next time she went to water the plant and got a whiff of the soil, but she was relieved to see her brother empty-handed again.

"That's better," Callie said, ignoring Veronica's friends, who were giggling nervously. She knew as well as anyone that Scott's biggest fault was that he could sometimes be a little too easygoing. He didn't always seem to realize that there could be consequences to just going with the flow all the time. "Now what do you say we get out of here?"

Scott raised one eyebrow in surprise. "You mean leave? Why? It's still early."

"He can't leave yet." Veronica grabbed Scott's arm and hugged it to her, smiling up at him. Now that the beer issue was settled, she seemed perfectly content again. "He's still got campaigning to do. Right, Scotty?"

"She's right." Scott reached over and gave Callie an apologetic pat on the shoulder. But his voice was firm. "I can't leave yet. It would be a waste of a perfect opportunity. The election's only ten days away, you know."

Callie scowled, but she didn't bother to argue. Her brother was easygoing all right, but he could be stubborn when he felt like it, too. "Fine," she muttered, not relishing the thought of watching the party degenerate even further. Still, she figured she'd better stick around and make sure Scott stayed out of trouble.

Veronica smirked at her briefly before turning back to Scott. It was perfectly obvious that she thought she had a lot to do with the fact that Scott was staying. And Callie didn't bother to disabuse her of that notion.

THIRTEEN

Half an hour later Lisa stopped her car at the curb in front of her house and sat in the darkened front seat with the key dangling from the ignition, wondering what to do. She had just dropped Emily off at her home across town, and now she had a decision to make.

She glanced at the front of her house. The upstairs windows were dark, but she could see flickering reddish light pouring onto the moonlit front lawn from the living room windows, which told her that her mother had lit a fire in the fireplace.

Next Lisa turned her gaze to the Lakes' house down the block, where lights were blazing from every window and the sound of the pounding music was faintly audible even here, inside her car with the doors and windows shut. She wondered if the beer had run out yet and how long it would take the drunken partyers to discover the liquor cabinet in the dining room.

I really wish Mr. and Mrs. Lake hadn't decided to go away this weekend, Lisa thought helplessly. *If they had been here, none of this would have happened and I wouldn't be sitting here trying to figure out how to deal with it.*

A car turned onto the block, and she automatically glanced up at it. With a gasp, she recognized Mrs. Lake's car. For one crazy second she thought her wish had come true and the Lakes had returned early from their trip. Then she remembered—Stevie's brother Chad and his friend had taken the car to drive to the bachelor party they were going to that evening. Lisa squinted at the windshield, though the headlights made it hard to see the figures in the front seat. Quickly unsnapping her seat belt, she jumped out of her car and waved them down.

Chad seemed surprised to see her and horrified when she told him what was going on at his house. "I totally forgot about those cases in the garage," he groaned, running both hands through his sandy hair. "We had so much other stuff that I didn't even notice they were missing. And after all the hassle we gave Stevie about keeping it cold . . ."

Luke, who had taken his time climbing out of

the car, was grinning. "Hey, it's no biggie," he said. "We had enough for ourselves even without it. I'm just glad we were able to make a contribution to the party."

Chad shot him an annoyed glance. "Zip it, Luke," he snapped. "This is major. My parents will slaughter us if they find out Stevie and her friends were drinking."

Lisa nodded, glad that Chad, at least, seemed to recognize the gravity of the situation. "So what do we do?"

"Let's go see how bad it is." Chad gestured at his car. "Come on, climb in."

Pausing just long enough to grab her keys and purse out of her own car, Lisa obeyed.

When Lisa, Chad, and Luke walked into the house, Lisa saw that things had gotten even wilder since she'd left. Someone had apparently discovered Mr. Lake's stash of oldies tapes, and the music was louder than ever, with dancers boogying on the sofa, in the hall, on the stairs—one petite girl was even dancing in her socks on the coffee table. Glancing around the living room, Lisa tried to spot her friends. Stevie wasn't hard to find. She and Julianna were dancing in a ragged circle around Phil and A.J., who were doing really bad impersonations of the Blues Brothers, complete with what had to be a couple of Mr. Lake's winter hats.

Oh well, at least maybe one good thing has come out of all this, Lisa thought grimly as she and Chad stood in the doorway. Luke had wandered off toward the kitchen. *At least Phil and A.J. seem to have made up.*

"Oh, man," Chad muttered, scanning the room. "This is worse than I thought."

Lisa nodded. She noticed that Callie was sitting on the sofa, deep in conversation with George Wheeler, both of them ignoring the chaos around them. Someone had turned on the TV, and Gary Korman and several of his friends were playing air guitar along with the video on MTV, which competed with the blaring stereo, making the whole house shudder with sound.

Chad nodded in the direction of the fireplace. "At least Carole doesn't seem to have gotten caught up in all this."

Turning to look, Lisa saw that Carole was standing with Scott and Veronica and several other people, none of whom were drinking. Despite the anger she still felt toward Carole, Lisa was relieved. At least not everyone had totally lost their minds.

Then her gaze shifted to the easy chair in the corner, and she gulped. Alex was sitting there, all alone, his head resting wearily on his hand. His earlier alcoholic euphoria had worn off, and he looked completely wiped out and miserable.

Before Lisa's mind had a chance to react, her heart went out to him. He looked so depressed, so exhausted—she just wanted to rush over to him, hold him, help him to feel better.

Then she remembered what had happened between them. She remembered the hurtful things he had said, the way he had refused to listen to her. She pictured him making a fool of himself by drooling all over Nicole.

Still, a part of her didn't care about any of that. That part just wanted to comfort him, to make things right any way possible. *Maybe I should go with my gut for once,* Lisa thought uncertainly, still hovering in the doorway. *Don't people always say that your first instinct is usually right? Well, my first instinct definitely told me to go over there. . . .*

She continued to waver as Chad walked on into the room, dodging the dancing crowds as he headed for his sister. Lisa hardly noticed his departure. All the unpleasant images from earlier that evening continued to parade through her head, making her dizzy.

I want to forget about our fight and move on, she thought desperately. *But he might not even want to see me—he might still be mad about the Skye thing. . . .*

Suddenly she realized something. It wasn't doing either of them any good for her to stand there and worry about the past, or about what Alex might or might not be thinking or feeling or wanting.

I can't control what he does, she told herself. *All I can do is take responsibility for my own actions. I'm not sure I've really been doing that so far.*

It was the first time she'd thought about it that way. Maybe Alex had been a little too jealous, maybe he hadn't trusted her as much as she thought he should, maybe he'd been too quick to blame her for everything. But she hadn't been exactly blameless, had she? She had kept secrets from him, including one really hurtful secret that went straight to the heart of his deepest fears. As hard as it would have been for him to hear what Skye had said at any time, it had been much worse to hear it so long after the fact—and from someone else, not her. She had no excuse for not telling him herself, and that meant that no matter what else had happened, she owed him an apology.

I've just got to forget about that other stuff, she thought, doing her best to push back all the memories of his jealous comments, his angry face as he'd confronted her, his drunken flirting, all the rest of it. *I've got to forget about that and deal with the real underlying problem between us. The problem that I started—and that I've got to fix before things go any further.*

Taking a deep breath, she headed toward him, determined to do her very best to set things right.

Stevie couldn't remember the last time she'd had so much fun. She always loved dancing, but that night the beat of the music seemed to fill her bones, throbbing through her and guiding her along in perfect harmony with every song.

This has got to be, without a doubt, the greatest party in the history of the universe, she exulted as Phil and A.J. sang along with the Blues Brothers at the top of their lungs. She giggled as they tried to execute some complicated dance steps and ended up almost tripping over their own feet. *Phil is so funny!* she thought gleefully. *A.J., too. They're really great. . . .*

"You guys are so great!" she cried, grabbing them both and giving them a big hug even as they danced. Julianna danced over to see what was going on, and Stevie pulled her into the hug, too. "You're great, too, Julie-jule-jule," she added fondly.

"Stevie."

Stevie gazed at Julianna in surprise. Had she just spoken? Her mouth hadn't even moved. Anyway, it couldn't have been her, could it? The voice that had said her name had sounded so deep, so stern. . . .

Feeling the pressure of a hand on her shoulder, she turned and saw her brother Chad standing there. A lightbulb blinked on in her head. Aha! So he was the one who had spoken to her. Mystery solved.

"Hi, big old baby big bro," she said, feeling a wave of love for her older brother wash over her. It was too bad he was away at college most of the time. "I'm so glad you're here! It wouldn't be a party without you."

"What's wrong with you, Stevie?" Chad replied bluntly. "I thought you knew better than this."

"Better than what?" Stevie giggled. She liked the way the words sounded, sort of like a little song. "Better than what? Better than what?"

"Shut up and listen to me," Chad said, grabbing her by both arms and glaring at her. "You've got to stop this drinking. If Mom and Dad find out you and your friends were boozing it up this way, they'll kill you—and me, too."

Stevie frowned. Why was Chad sounding so

uptight? He had gone to a party with beer, and he was no more legal than she was. Was he? She knew he was definitely older than her, but beyond that the details got a little hazy, and she didn't feel like stopping to figure it out just then. But in any case, she *did* know that the only reason there was beer at her party was because he'd carelessly left it behind. So where did he get off lecturing her? "Don't worry about it," she told him. "I can handle it. It's no big deal."

"It *is* a big deal!" Chad exclaimed. "You're sixteen years old! And in case you didn't notice, half the people here are wasted."

"Oh, come on." Stevie glanced around. She was sure he had to be exaggerating. For one thing, she and her friends certainly weren't wasted. She herself had only had a couple of beers, and she didn't even feel that drunk. The alcohol had just made her relax a little, made her forget all her worries about that boring election business and helped her have fun. Which reminded her . . .

Her shoulders started to sway again as a new song came on. Every minute she wasted arguing with Chad was a minute she could be spending dancing her head off.

"Whatever," she told her brother serenely.

"Let's talk about this later, okay? Right now I've got some serious partying to—"

The end of her sentence was lost in a sudden loud pounding from somewhere in the direction of the hall, audible even above the almost deafening cacophony of stereo and TV. Stevie jumped. Her friends stopped dancing, and Chad spun around to look.

"What was that?" Stevie asked, hoping that nobody had knocked over anything important.

Before Chad or the others could answer, the pounding came again. "Open up!" a muffled but authoritative voice shouted. "Police!"

FOURTEEN

An hour later, it was all over except for the cleanup.

"I can't believe the cops got everyone out of here so fast," Stevie muttered as she poked her foot at a pile of empty plastic cups in the hallway.

Chad shot her a grim glance as he bent to retrieve the hall rug, which someone had apparently used as a kind of skateboard, leaving it wadded against the foot of the stairs. "I'm just glad they made sure nobody who was drinking drove themselves home. I feel guilty enough about this whole situation without any car crashes on my conscience." The police had given rides to a few of the partyers themselves and called some parents to pick up others.

A groan from the direction of the living room reminded Stevie that she and Chad weren't alone. She poked her head into the room. Alex was sprawled on the sofa, holding his head and looking as ill as Stevie had ever seen him. "Are you okay?" she asked worriedly. "Should I get a bucket or something?"

Not that it would make much of a difference if he barfed all over the couch, she thought ruefully, glancing around at the disaster area that had once been their living room. *This place isn't going to be appearing in any decorating magazines anytime soon either way.* Cups and paper plates and shredded napkins were scattered everywhere. Most of the chair cushions were on the floor, and at least one of them was sporting a large black footprint. There was a large, sticky wet patch on one chair that she guessed was fruit punch, and someone seemed to have stomped several brownies into the carpet in front of the fireplace. CD and tape cases were lying open here and there, and it was anybody's guess where their contents had gone. Someone had even drawn a smiley face on the TV screen with bright pink lipstick.

Stevie glanced back at Alex. Judging by the way he was clutching his forehead with both hands, his head had to be throbbing even more than hers was. The arrival of the police had sobered her up pretty quickly, but she could still feel a heaviness just behind her eyes that she was sure would eventually resolve itself into a pounding headache. Her limbs felt strangely heavy, too, almost numb, and her mouth seemed to have grown some kind of invisible fungus over every surface, making her teeth feel mummified. Even so, she could tell she was in much better shape than her twin, and she found herself wondering just how many beers he'd had.

He was on his second or third when I went outside and found him, she thought, trying to piece together her fragmented memories of the evening. *Then we had one or maybe two together before we went back in, and he and A.J. went to get refills right after that, and then I think he chugged a couple with Phil when A.J. dared them to that time, and then—*

"Hey, Stevie," Chad interrupted her thoughts as he called to her from the hall, sounding annoyed. "Are you just going to stand there and leave me to clean this place up by myself?"

"Sorry," Stevie said guiltily. "Um, but do you think maybe we should put Alex to bed first? He doesn't look too good."

Chad joined her in the living room. "Hmmm, I guess you're right," he said, walking over and staring down at Alex with his hands on his hips. "He's not going to be much help anyway."

With some difficulty, they managed to get

Alex onto his feet and up the stairs. He moaned and groaned the entire time, but when his siblings lowered him onto his bed, he suddenly smiled.

"What?" Stevie panted, exhausted from helping drag and shove him all the way to his room. "What are you looking so happy about?"

Alex waved a hand weakly at his bedside table. Turning, Stevie saw a framed photo of Lisa smiling back at her. "Lisa and I—we made up," Alex mumbled. The smile had already faded, and his eyes drifted shut. "We're back together."

Chad shrugged and rolled his eyes. But Stevie was surprised and glad at the bit of good news, which might have been the only bright spot in the sea of gloom that her life had suddenly become. She wondered briefly what had happened to bring the couple back together, but one look at Chad's irritated face sent thoughts of asking scurrying away.

I'll have plenty of time to talk to Alex about Lisa when we're grounded for the rest of our lives, she thought grimly. *If I don't want to be shipped off to military school on top of it, I guess I'd better get to work.*

The thought of trying to put the house back together before her parents returned early the next morning—the police had called the Lakes at their hotel in New York to tell them what had happened—made her feel even more exhausted than she'd already felt. But she knew she didn't have any choice.

"Come on," she told Chad. "We might as well start in the living room. That could take us the rest of the night."

"Good." Chad glanced at her as they left Alex's room and headed for the stairs. "Because I have a lot I want to say to you."

Stevie groaned. "Can't the brotherly lectures wait?" she begged. "My head hurts as it is."

"Even better," Chad said again. "Maybe the next time you think about getting wasted, you'll remember how it felt and change your mind."

Stevie grabbed the banister, not completely trusting her legs, which felt a little wobbly. "Don't worry," she assured her brother. "I won't make this mistake again anytime soon, that's for sure." She shrugged. "I'm not even sure how it happened this time."

"I was pretty surprised myself." Chad gave her an appraising look as they reached the bottom of the stairs and headed into the living room together. "I have to admit, Stevie, I never thought you were the type to give in to peer pressure. I thought you were, you know, stronger than that."

Stevie tried to work up some indignation at the comment, but she couldn't quite manage it. "It was an accident," she said quietly as she stooped to pick up a crumpled potato chip bag. "I found Alex and A.J. drinking outside, and I didn't want them to go inside where people would see the beer because—" She shrugged wearily and glanced around the messy room. "Well, because I didn't want *this* to happen."

"Let me get this straight." Chad cocked an eyebrow at her. "You were trying to stop Alex from drinking, so you decided to get drunk yourself."

She had to admit that it sounded pretty stupid when he put it like that. "It made sense at the time," she said weakly. "I mean, they dared me, and I was just trying to buy some time—I was just going to play along, have a few sips to keep them happy while I tried to figure out how to convince them to lay off. But somehow, after those first few sips—"

"It didn't seem like a big deal anymore," Chad finished for her. He grimaced and tossed part of a broken juice glass onto the pile of trash that was growing as they talked. "Classic. Absolutely classic. You have no tolerance for alcohol, but you go ahead and have that first drink anyway because you think you can handle it. Instead, it goes straight to your head and makes you think another drink sounds awfully good, and so on and so forth." He sighed. "We've all been there, I guess."

"Well, whatever." Stevie didn't particularly like the idea that her behavior that night had followed some kind of predictable, common pattern, as Chad seemed to be saying, but she didn't have the energy to argue. "Anyway, after a few minutes I guess I sort of forgot about trying to stop Alex and A.J." She shuddered as a few more disjointed, fuzzy memories bubbled up slowly from earlier that evening. "Actually, I think it may have been my idea to go inside. And I'm pretty sure I was the one who convinced Phil to join in. He was really thirsty from dancing with Emily—" She gasped. "Emily! What happened to her, anyway? I didn't see her when the police came."

Chad shrugged. Stevie felt more terrible than ever as she realized that what had started as Emily's special night had ended in such disaster. *I just hope that someday, after she's spent years and years in Australia and has forgotten some of what happened, she'll manage to find it in her heart to forgive me for this,* she thought sadly. *I hope this won't end up being her strongest memory of her friends in Willow Creek.*

There was nothing she could do about Emily at the moment, though, except to hope that she'd found her way home safely. Stretching to grab someone's sock off the top of the bookshelf, Stevie glanced at Chad. "Anyway, as I was saying, I talked Phil into having a beer. Then we were dancing, and getting hot and thirsty, and drinking some more, and having so much fun, especially since A.J. wasn't upset anymore and we were all friends again. . . ."

"I know." Chad shot her a sympathetic look. "Hey, like I said, I've been there. I wish you hadn't done it, but I guess it's not totally your fault. If Luke and I hadn't left that beer here—"

"Don't blame yourself," Stevie said quickly, not wanting her brother to feel guilty because of something she and her friends had done. "Just because it was here didn't mean we had to drink it."

"Get real." Chad shook his head. "I told Mom and Dad I'd keep an eye on things, and instead I ended up helping a bunch of high-schoolers get drunk."

Stevie shook her head, though she immediately regretted it when her vision started to swim crazily. Blinking to straighten out the world again, she glanced more carefully at Chad. "You weren't responsible for baby-sitting us," she reminded him, hating the disappointment and guilt she saw written all over his face. "Anyway, it was just as much that jerk Luke's fault as yours." Luke had slipped out when the police had arrived, apparently deciding either to drive back to school or to find another friend to crash with, since his car had disappeared from the curb in front of their house. "I wish he hadn't split on us," Stevie grumbled, feeling more than a little sorry for herself as she peeled a wad of chewing gum off her mother's favorite antique end table. "We could use his help right about now."

"Luke's not the kind of guy to stick around and deal with consequences if he can find an escape route," Chad said ruefully. "He didn't think the party was any big deal before the cops showed up. But he probably decided to make himself scarce when he realized that, technically, he was the one who supplied beer to all those minors, even if it was an accident."

"Lucky him." Stevie ran her tongue over her teeth, which were feeling furrier and more disgusting than ever. She was also feeling guiltier than ever about what had happened. It was just sinking in exactly how many people were going to be affected by what had happened that night. People she cared about. "I have a feeling the rest of us are going to be dealing with consequences for quite some time."

In her kitchen at home, Carole was trying to keep her eyes open as her father continued the stern speech that he had begun a half hour earlier when she had arrived home from the party. Since she hadn't been drinking, the police had let her drive herself home, and she'd ended up pulling into the driveway right behind her father, who was returning from a black-tie benefit dinner in Washington. His jovial queries about her evening had quickly changed to grim, tense questions when Carole had admitted what had happened at the party.

She'd known there was no point in trying to keep it from him—even though the police hadn't called the parents of anyone they didn't catch drinking, there was no doubt that the full story would be all over town by the next morning at the latest. Not that Carole would have lied in any case—after suffering alone through the guilt about her history test, she'd vowed never to hide anything from her father again. Ever since her mother had died, leaving the two of them with only each other to lean on, she'd confided in him about almost everything important that happened in her life. Knowing that she would never be able to tell him she'd cheated on that test had left a lonely hole in her soul that she had no intention of making larger with more lies.

Besides, who would have thought he'd freak out like this? she thought as her father listed all the people he'd ever known or heard of who'd been killed in drunk driving accidents. *I mean, you'd think he would be proud of me or something. I resisted peer pressure. I didn't touch a drop of beer. So what's he getting so worked up about?*

"Carole," Colonel Hanson said sharply. "Are you listening to me?"

Carole realized that her head, which was resting heavily on her hand, was drooping toward the kitchen table. "Sorry." She blinked at him and bit back a yawn. "I'm listening, really. I'm just getting kind of tired."

Colonel Hanson glanced at the clock on the microwave oven and sighed. "No, I'm sorry, sweetie," he said. "It's really late, and I know you must be exhausted. I am, too. But I just want to make sure you realize how serious this all is."

"I know, Dad."

"I'm glad you didn't drink," he went on. "But I don't like the thought that you ended up at that kind of party at all. I hope you're going to spend some time thinking about what could have happened if the police hadn't intervened. I know that when you're young, it doesn't seem as though anything bad could ever happen to you or your friends, but . . ."

Carole's mind drifted off again as her father rambled on, his brow furrowed and his eyes distant and serious. *I know he means well,* she thought. *And I guess I don't blame him for being worried and all that. But I never would have guessed he'd be so riled up that he won't even let me go to bed when it's the middle of the night.* She shuddered slightly as her mind wandered back to that history test yet again. *I mean, if he's reacting this strongly about something I* didn't *do and admitted to, I can't even imagine how he would react if he ever found out about what I* did *do and kept a secret. I guess it's a really good thing I haven't told him about that stupid test.*

She bit her lip. Part of her still wished she could just blurt out the whole story of the test right then and there. It would feel so good to get it off her chest. . . .

But she knew it was never going to happen. Now more than ever, she was aware that at this point, telling her father would be an absolute disaster. *Just look at where Lisa's secrets got her,* she thought, remembering how a few careless words had cost her friend her relationship. It gave her a desolate, empty feeling to think that her own relationship with Lisa might be damaged beyond repair, in addition to the guilt she felt about ruining things for Lisa and Alex. *If I'd never opened my big mouth, Alex would never have needed to know about the thing with Skye. And he and Lisa would still be together.*

I'm so glad that Alex and I are back together, Lisa thought pensively as she lay in bed, staring at the shadow of the tree outside her window, which was silhouetted against her ceiling by the milky white light of the moon.

She'd been lying there for almost an hour, feeling exhausted but much too overwhelmed to sleep. Thankfully, Rafe had already left by the time she'd arrived home from the party, and her mother had been too giddy about her own evening to pry much into her daughter's. Lisa knew that her mother would hear about what had happened sooner or later—probably sooner—but she would just have to deal with that when the time came. Right now she had more important things to think about.

When Alex had accepted her apology and agreed to try to work things out, at first Lisa had been so relieved that she'd hardly thought about what that meant. But now it was all she could think about.

I still can't believe how he acted tonight after our fight, running off and getting drunk and stupid, she thought, idly tracing the raised rose pattern of her comforter with her fingertips. *I've never seen him like that before. I wouldn't have expected it from him.*

She didn't like remembering what he had been like under the influence of all that beer. It had been almost as if Alex—her beloved, familiar Alex—had disappeared, replaced by a complete stranger. Even though they were back together now, remembering the shock of seeing him that way made her feel somehow more separate from him than ever. She still had no doubt that she loved him, or that he loved her. She was glad that their relationship was on the mend. But she couldn't help thinking that things between them would never be quite the same again.

Too many things have happened that we can't take back, she realized, still staring fixedly at the ceiling. *On both sides. My secrets and lies, his jealousy and suspicion, and now, on top of it all, the memory of how he acted when he was drinking. . . . I'll never be able to look at that girl Nicole again without seeing him running his hands over her hair and kissing her. . . .*

She shuddered, willing the image away. No, it certainly wasn't going to be easy to forget that. But she had to try. She didn't have a choice, not if she wanted to get through this with her relationship intact.

All I can do is make sure it doesn't happen again, she thought, making a firm decision to do just that. *From now on I'll have to be honest with Alex, even if I'm sometimes scared about how he'll react. If I want him to trust me, I have to trust him to love me no matter what. And I have to remember that no one can be responsible for anyone else's actions or thoughts or feelings. Only their own.*

That reminded her of her friends. Carole and Stevie had both been caught up in Lisa's secrets, and they had both ended up suffering for it. Carole had made what Lisa realized now had to have been an innocent mistake, and Lisa had turned her into a scapegoat for her own failings. Meanwhile, Stevie had been put on the spot, forced to divide her loyalties between her twin and one of her best friends.

I haven't been fair to either of them. Lisa closed her eyes, feeling sleep beginning to creep up on her at last. *I'll definitely have to see what I can do about that tomorrow . . .*

FIFTEEN

On Sunday morning, for the first time in her life, Carole was tempted to call in sick to her job at Pine Hollow. For one thing, she had gotten only about four hours of sleep after her father had finally finished his lecture on the evils of alcohol, and she could barely keep her eyes open. For another, she couldn't bear the thought of having to face Ben—not yet, and maybe not ever. Sunday was his day off, at least officially, but more often than not he ended up coming to the stable anyway.

In the end, though, her sense of responsibility won out and she cautiously entered the stable building at her usual time. Hurrying directly to the office, she quickly ascertained that Ben's jacket wasn't in its usual place on the hook on the back of the door.

"Thank goodness," she muttered, relieved. He was almost always the first to arrive in the morning, so if he hadn't showed up yet, he wasn't likely to show up at all. For a second she wondered if the chance of seeing her had anything to do with his staying away, but she did her best to banish the thought.

As she slipped her feet into the work boots she kept under the desk, she heard Max calling for someone to help him with some hay bales, and she threw herself into her work. Unpleasant thoughts of Ben and the party faded slightly as she raced through her stable chores, and they receded completely into the background a couple of hours later when she finally tightened Samson's girth and climbed into the big black horse's saddle to start his daily training session.

The thoughts all came crashing back, however, when she walked into the tack room after the session with Samson's sweaty saddle and bridle and found herself face to face with Lisa. "Oh," Carole said, her heart starting to pound. "Um, hi."

To her surprise, Lisa gave her a civil nod. "Hi." Her voice was neutral.

Before Carole could figure out what that meant, Stevie came barreling into the room. She stopped short when she saw her friends standing there. "Oops," she said quickly. "Uh, I didn't know anybody was in here."

For a long second there was silence. Carole could feel her face turning red as she searched her mind for something to say. All she kept coming back to was the fervent wish that she could wave a magic wand and put everything back to the way it was before. Before she had ruined Lisa's life. Before she'd babbled like a fool and made Stevie's brother miserable.

The awkward moment was shattered when Max's five-year-old daughter, Maxi, raced in. "Hey!" the little girl cried when she spotted them. "Carole, Lisa, Stevie. Daddy needs to talk to you. He says I'm s'posed to tell you to hurry, hurry, hurry."

Prancer. Carole's first thought was for the pregnant mare. She hadn't seen Judy Barker yet that day, but the vet had promised to stop by and check on Prancer's condition if she could. "Where is he?" Carole asked Maxi urgently.

"Prancer's stall." The little girl skipped out of the room without waiting around for any more questions. The three older girls raced out after her, passing her in the hall and hurrying on toward the big box stall where Prancer spent most of her time.

Lisa's heart was in her throat as she rounded the corner and came within sight of the stall. With everything that had happened at the party the night before, her worries about Prancer had slipped to the back of her mind. But today they were back, and little Maxi's orders to *hurry, hurry, hurry* had sent an icy chill skittering down her spine.

After everything else that's happened, I don't think I can take any more bad news, she told herself fearfully. *I don't think I could stand it.*

Max and Judy were standing just outside Prancer's stall when the girls reached them. Max didn't keep them in suspense for long.

"Good news, girls," he called as soon as he spotted them. "Judy just checked, and both foals' heartbeats are pumping along nice and steady."

Lisa collapsed against the nearest support beam with relief. "Are you sure?"

"Positive," Judy replied, snapping her black medical bag shut. "The babies are both fine, and so is Mama."

"Whew!" Stevie exclaimed, speaking for all of them.

Feeling a little weak in the knees, Lisa walked over to the stall to pat Prancer, who had her head out over the door and was watching the humans with her calm, unreadable dark eyes. Stroking the mare's neck, Lisa felt her barely repressed fears melting away. She knew she couldn't really relax completely—Prancer still had a long, difficult road in front of her, and Lisa knew that it would be remarkable if she wound up at the end of it with two healthy foals—but this was certainly a step in the right direction. They all deserved to be happy about it.

Max and Judy said good-bye and wandered off around the corner, discussing a yearling that needed some inoculations and leaving the three girls alone in the aisle. Lisa was feeling so grateful about Prancer's positive diagnosis that she found new strength in her resolve to make things right with her friends. Seeing Carole back in the tack room had startled her, reminding her as it did of what had happened. But she had recovered her wits now—she was ready to talk.

"Listen," she said, turning to Carole first. "I want to say something. I'm really sorry about the way I yelled at you yesterday. I hope you can forgive me."

Carole looked astonished. "Me forgive you?" she blurted out. "Are you kidding? I was just trying to figure out how to ask *you* to forgive *me*. I mean, I totally ruined your life."

"Not really." Lisa smiled tentatively. "Alex and I are going to be okay. We made up last night just before the party, um, ended."

"You mean before the big police raid," Stevie corrected dryly.

"Whatever." Lisa put out a hand toward Carole. "Anyway, do you think we can forget about all that?"

"I hope not," Carole replied truthfully, taking her friend's hand and squeezing it. "I want to remember it so that I don't make the same kind of mistake again. But I can forgive it all if you can. Both of you." She glanced at Stevie, who looked rather surprised.

"Me? What do I have to forgive?"

"You could forgive *me* for putting you in the middle of me and Alex," Lisa said. "I wish I'd never asked you to keep that secret from him." She grimaced. "I wish I'd never had any secrets to begin with. The last couple of months would have been a whole lot easier if I hadn't had that on my mind all the time."

Carole glanced at Prancer, who was resting her big head on Lisa's shoulder as the girls talked, and said, "Well, maybe not totally easy."

Lisa smiled ruefully. That was the truth. It had been a busy autumn any way you looked at it. But that didn't change what she was trying to say. "Right. But anyway, I just want to tell you both right now—from this day forward, I'm going to be as truthful as I can be. And part of that means trying to trust other people more, too." She shrugged. "For instance, I'll try to trust people to handle it when I tell them the truth."

"If we're making vows here, I've got one." Carole's dark eyes were earnest. "I'm going to try to start thinking more before I speak. Especially when what I'm speaking about is other people's lives."

Stevie was happy that her friends were making up. It wasn't easy to see two people she cared about angry with each other the way Lisa and Carole had been the night before. Or the way Lisa and Alex had been when they'd broken up. Being in the middle was tough because it often meant she was pulled in two directions at once without really being able to do anything to help. But she supposed she would just have to get better at dealing with it.

"Okay," she said briskly. "So does this mean everybody's forgiven everybody and we're all friends again?"

"I hope so," Lisa said. "Carole?"

Carole nodded, smiling shyly. "Definitely."

"Good." Stevie spread her arms. "Then come on. Three-way hug time!"

The three of them wrapped their arms around each other and squeezed tight for a long minute before coming apart again. When they did, suddenly the tenseness that had existed among them just moments before had disappeared.

Carole hated to interrupt their reunion, but she suddenly remembered that she was supposed to be working. "I'd better get back to the tack room before Max notices the dirty saddle and bridle I left there," she said. "Want to come keep me company?"

"Sure," Stevie and Lisa said in unison.

"I can't stay long, though," Stevie added as they wandered back down the aisle. "I'm technically grounded right now, and if I'm not home in an hour, Mom and Dad will probably send out the National Guard to drag me there."

Carole gasped. "I forgot to ask!" she exclaimed. "What happened after the rest of us left last night?"

"You don't want to know." Stevie rolled her eyes. "By the time the cops called my parents, it was too late for them to get a train home. But they rushed down here first thing this morning and didn't stop yelling for about three hours. Maybe four. The only one worse off than me is Alex. He's totally hung over today, and I don't think all that yelling helped his headache one bit."

"How long are you grounded for?" Carole asked.

Stevie sighed as the three girls entered the tack room. "They didn't exactly say," she said. "All they would promise was to discuss letting us off sometime after the holidays. I just hope the holidays they're talking about aren't Memorial Day and the Fourth of July."

"So if you're grounded, what are you doing here now?" asked Lisa, logical as always.

"Fortunately, they decided that in my case, the Colesford Horse Show is an exception to my grounding. I'm still allowed to be in it, which means they kind of have to let me keep training for it."

"Wow." Lisa looked surprised. "That was nice of them." *A miracle is more like it,* she added privately. Stevie's parents were kind, easygoing people most of the time. But they could be strict when they wanted to be—really strict.

"Maybe. Personally, I think it's probably only because they know Max is counting on me—and has already paid my entry fees." Stevie shrugged. "But hey, I'm not about to look a gift horse in the mouth. So to speak."

Carole had already set to work scrubbing Samson's tack, but she glanced up from her task. "Whatever the reason, I'm glad you can still be in the show," she said.

Stevie picked up some saddle soap and started

helping Carole. "Me too. But I don't want you to get the wrong idea and think that my parents took this well." She shook her head ruefully, still hearing the echoes of her father's yelling in her ears and seeing the shadow of her mother's disappointed expression. "They didn't. They're really furious at the three of us—me, Alex, and Chad. While we're grounded, Alex and I have to do all sorts of work around the house to earn the money to pay them back for the stuff that got damaged. We convinced them that Chad shouldn't have to chip in since it wasn't really his fault, but they're still not exactly happy with him right now." She sighed. "I think it will be a really long time before they trust any of us again."

Carole nodded, understanding exactly what she meant. But another question was tugging at her mind, stirring her curiosity. She cleared her throat. "Listen, Stevie," she began hesitantly. "When you—I mean, what was it like, um, you know. When you were—well—"

"When I was drunk? Wasted? Blotto? Soused?" Stevie asked bluntly. "You can say the words."

"Okay, then," Lisa said. "I'm curious, too. What was it like to get drunk?"

Stevie looked pensive. "It's kind of hard to

describe," she said. "At first I didn't think it was affecting me. I mean, I was sipping that first beer, and really I was just trying to figure out what to do about Alex and A.J. Then I realized the can was almost empty, and I remember thinking, *Wow, that didn't do anything at all.*" She tossed the saddle soap she'd been using back into the bucket in the corner. "But gradually I starting thinking that maybe what Alex and A.J. were doing wasn't such a big problem after all. And while I was thinking that, A.J. handed me a second beer and I just sort of automatically opened it. I took a small sip, and it tasted really good, even though I hadn't really liked the taste at first. And I couldn't really think of a reason not to keep drinking, since I didn't think it was affecting me. . . ."

"Sounds like it was, though," Lisa commented.

"I realize that now," Stevie agreed. "But I'm just telling you what I was thinking at the time. One thing I know I *wasn't* thinking about was the fact that I'd barely eaten a thing all day because I was so busy getting ready for the party and that even a few sips of beer would go straight to my head."

"Yikes," Carole said. "No wonder it happened so fast."

Stevie nodded. "It really did. Before I knew it, I was so buzzed that I'd forgotten all about everything I'd been worried about, and all I could think of was how much I wanted to go inside and give Phil a big hug and do some serious dancing. So the three of us went in, and the rest is history."

"Wow." Carole shook her head, trying to imagine what it would be like to do what Stevie had done. She wasn't sure she wanted to find out anytime soon. She still couldn't shake the memory of Alex's sloppy attempt to kiss her, or the way A.J. had kept crashing into things while he danced, hardly seeming to notice as he knocked over furniture and spilled food and drinks all over the place. It had been scary to see people she knew so far out of control. She only hoped that Alex didn't remember the kissing incident now that he was sober again. "You seem all right today, at least," she told Stevie, looking for whatever bright side she could find in the situation.

"I'm okay," Stevie said. "My stomach still feels a little queasy and I'm really tired, but otherwise I'll live. Alex, on the other hand . . ."

"I know," Lisa put in. "I spoke to him this morning before I came over here. He didn't sound too good."

Stevie grimaced. "No kidding. He was up half the night hurling his guts up into the toilet. This morning he barely managed to choke down a piece of toast before he headed back upstairs to take some aspirin, drink three gallons of water, and go back to bed."

"Poor guy." Carole felt terrible for Alex, especially since she still felt responsible for the way he'd ended up. If she hadn't opened her mouth about Skye, and if he and Lisa hadn't had that fight as a result, then maybe he wouldn't have been tempted to drink. Maybe instead he and Stevie would have made A.J. put the beer away, and the whole disaster wouldn't have happened.

She shook her head. If she kept thinking that way, she'd go nuts. This wasn't like that botched history test, where she had brought everything on herself. Maybe she had made a mistake this time, but other people had made some really bad choices, too. She hadn't forced them to make those choices, any more than her history teacher had forced her to cheat by giving her a retest. Everyone had to live with the consequences of their own actions.

"So you and Alex are okay now?" she asked Lisa tentatively.

"More or less," Lisa replied. "I know we both have a lot of work to do to get our relationship back on track. But we're both willing to try, and I guess that's half the battle. I hope so, anyway."

"Alex said you're coming over later to talk," Stevie said.

Lisa nodded. "We're going to spend the afternoon figuring out where to go from here. Your parents weren't going to let me come over since he's grounded, but I guess they figured we wouldn't have much fun, considering his current condition."

"I'm sure that's part of it," Stevie agreed. "But I overheard them talking after breakfast, and I think it's also because they know you didn't drink last night. They're probably hoping you're going to help them yell at him."

Lisa smiled, but she felt her stomach flip-flop as she thought about the conversation to come. She and Alex had a lot to say to each other, and not all of it was going to be easy. They had to learn to trust each other more, but already she felt as though she had a secret hanging over her head.

How am I going to tell him that I'm going to California for Thanksgiving? she wondered. *He probably still thinks I'm spending the holiday with him. And why shouldn't he? I told him I would.*

When she'd called her father that morning, hoping to explain things to him and beg off the trip, she'd found that she'd been too late. Even before she'd said a word about Thanksgiving, her father had proudly announced that he'd gone online the night before right after she'd called and bought her a plane ticket over the Internet. Because it was for a holiday weekend, the ticket was nonrefundable, which he'd turned into a joke about how he'd trapped her into coming to visit. Lisa had swallowed all her excuses and explanations, realizing that she really was trapped, and had done her best to fake happiness at his news.

Oh, well, she thought apprehensively. *Alex will just have to understand.*

Callie felt a bit wistful as she left Max's office. She had just stopped in for a quick discussion of her therapeutic riding schedule for the next couple of weeks. It was strange to think of continuing her sessions without Emily, who was spending the next couple of days packing and tying up the loose ends of her life in Willow Creek before flying off to her new life in Australia on Tuesday.

But Callie wasn't the type to waste a lot of time wishing that things were different. She would miss Emily like crazy, but she had to move on. She had finished her first solo session that morning aboard Patch, one of Pine Hollow's gentlest school horses, and it had gone pretty well.

As she walked past the tack room on her way to the locker room, where she was supposed to meet Scott, she saw Stevie, Carole, and Lisa emerging. To her relief, it appeared that the three of them were friends again despite everything that had happened the night before.

Stevie spotted her first. "Callie!" she said. "Hi there. How's it going?"

"Okay." Callie couldn't help sighing. "Well, mostly, anyway. I miss Emily already, even though she hasn't even left yet."

"Me too," Carole said, and Lisa nodded agreement.

Stevie rubbed her forehead. "I miss her too, but I doubt she's going to miss me much after what happened last night."

"I'm sure she won't hold it against you," Callie said tactfully. She was dying for more details about the party's aftermath, but first she had to get something off her chest. "Actually, though, speaking of guilty feelings, I want to apologize for the way Scott and I ducked out last night when the police turned up."

"I'm glad you did," Stevie said. "I never would have forgiven myself if the party that was supposed to be Scott's ticket to victory in the election had ended up destroying his chances."

"That's what Veronica was worried about, too," Callie admitted. "It was actually her idea to scoot out the kitchen door. Thanks to her quick thinking, we got away clean." She shuddered as she remembered the close call. Scott had only had a few sips of beer, but he'd still had the scent on his breath. If the cops had smelled it and called their parents . . . She broke off the thought as she noticed that Stevie looked slightly disgruntled. "Are you sure you're not mad?"

"Not at you," Stevie assured her. "I know you have to be totally careful because of who your father is and all that. No, the only one I'm mad at is Veronica."

"Why?" Lisa looked surprised. "Callie just said that she was the one who got them out and saved Scott from being caught."

Stevie scowled. "I know. That's the problem. I hate being grateful to a snake like Veronica."

Callie smiled. She hadn't been around for most of the years that Stevie and Veronica had known each other, but she'd heard enough stories to know that the two of them had never exactly been bosom buddies. "Well, then you're really going to hate this," she said. "Veronica has promised to be Scott's alibi in case any of his political opponents get wind of what happened and try to use it against him. Everyone in school knows she doesn't drink and doesn't tolerate anyone who does."

"And besides, nobody will want the hassle of arguing with her." Stevie cracked a grudging smile. "Well, she's a pain in the butt, but I guess she does have her uses." She cleared her throat. "As it turned out, she even managed to do some good while she was hanging all over Scott last night. I thought she'd end up monopolizing his attention, but instead she made the rounds with him, talking him up to everyone she knew."

"Does this mean you're thinking of taking her on as your assistant campaign manager?" Carole teased.

Stevie snorted. "Hardly," she declared.

At that moment, Scott himself appeared at the end of the hallway and hurried toward them. "Hi, everyone. What are you all doing hiding out back here?"

"Talking about you," Stevie replied pertly.

"Really?" Scott grinned. "May I join in? That's my favorite topic."

Callie rolled her eyes as the others laughed. "Actually, we were talking more about your new shadow, Veronica," she told her brother.

"Oh, in that case, I should probably let you

know"—he turned to Stevie—"Ronnie had some really fantastic ideas last night for issues we could talk up before the election."

Stevie wasn't sure she liked the sound of that. "*Veronica*? Really? Like what?"

Scott scratched his chin thoughtfully. "Let me see. For one thing, she thinks that we ought to jump on the bandwagon on that school dance idea a couple of the other candidates have mentioned. She thinks it's an issue that everyone will care about, that it could make the difference in a close race, and I'm not sure she isn't right about that. And she isn't sure we should focus so much on the class budget stuff, since most people really don't—"

"Whatever," Stevie cut in. She was a little annoyed that Veronica was second-guessing her campaign strategy—and that Scott actually seemed to be listening—but she didn't want to get into it right then. She noticed Carole and Lisa exchanging glances and guessed they had sensed her irritation, but fortunately Scott seemed unaware that anything was wrong. "We can talk about it at school tomorrow, okay?"

"Okay," Scott agreed cheerfully. "I'll make a list, and maybe we can go over it before chemistry."

"Fine." Stevie didn't bother to tell him that

most of "Ronnie's" ideas were probably worthless. She would talk some sense into Scott tomorrow—after all, she was still his campaign manager, whatever delusions of grandeur Veronica might have.

Scott glanced at his sister. "Ready to go, Callie?" He grinned. "Or do you need to stick around for some more girl talk about your big date next weekend?"

Stevie's eyes widened with sudden curiosity as Callie shot her brother a sour look. "What's this?" Stevie cried. "Callie, is there something you've neglected to tell us?"

Lisa felt curious too, suddenly remembering her last view of Callie at the party, talking earnestly with George Wheeler. But she knew that Callie was a very private person, and she didn't think it was fair for them to put her on the spot. "You don't have to tell us if you don't—" she began tactfully, but Stevie cut her off.

"Don't be ridiculous," she snapped. "Of course she has to tell us. I'm grounded for the rest of my life, remember? The only joy I'll have from now on is hearing about what other people are doing."

Scott looked abashed. "Sorry, sis," he told Callie. "I didn't realize you hadn't said anything about it."

"It's okay." Callie played absently with the ends of her long blond hair, not meeting anyone's eye. "I hadn't said anything because I haven't decided what to do about him yet."

"Who?" Carole asked. "I mean, sorry to pry, but . . ."

"George," Callie replied frankly. "George Wheeler. He's the one who asked me out. He wants to take me to dinner next Saturday night."

"That's nice." Stevie was doing her best to keep her voice neutral, but she was burning to know more. Once the party had started she had almost completely forgotten about George's crush on Callie—she'd meant to keep an eye on the two of them to see what happened, but more pressing matters had intervened. "Um, so you're not sure you're going to go out with him?"

Callie shrugged helplessly. "I'm not sure about anything," she admitted. "I mean, I had a really nice time dancing with him and talking to him last night. And he's nice and smart and everything. . . . But I'm just not sure I see him that way, you know?"

Stevie knew exactly what she meant. But she also knew how bad George had it for Callie, and she hated to think how hurt he would be if she didn't even give him a chance. "I understand completely," she said brightly. "Still, what's the worst that could happen if you went out with him just this once? At least you'd get a nice dinner out of it."

"True."

Callie still looked uncertain, and Stevie could tell she wasn't ready to make up her mind yet. "Well, good luck either way," she said, glancing at her watch. "And I hate to say it, but I think I'd better run. I don't want to tee off the folks on my first day of grounding or they'll never parole me."

As they all said their good-byes and parted ways, Carole was still thinking idly about Callie's news. Somehow, people's romantic lives always seemed to take her by surprise. As she grabbed a pitchfork out of the tool closet and wandered down the stable aisle, she did her best to imagine what might have happened between Callie and George, what conversations they'd had to bring them to this point. But whatever she did, she couldn't quite picture beautiful, elegant, self-possessed Callie actually going out with shy, bumbling, pudgy George.

Suddenly her heart stopped as she recognized a familiar head of shaggy dark hair at the far end of the aisle. *Then again,* she told herself as she dodged into the nearest stall to avoid being spotted by Ben, who had apparently showed up at the stable that day after all, *I don't exactly have the best instincts about that sort of thing.*

She was thinking about the embarrassing incident with Ben, but she was also thinking about her ill-advised comment to Alex. Somehow, she always felt as if she was about three steps behind everyone else when it came to romantic relationships. She never quite knew what was expected of her or why other people did some of the things they did.

Her thoughts were interrupted by the pressure of a soft nose shoving gently at her shoulder. Turning, she realized for the first time that the stall she was hiding in was Prancer's.

"Hi, girl," she murmured, rubbing the mare's head and then slipping her arms around her neck for a hug. "What do you think? Do you know why people never act the way I expect them to?"

The mare merely let her eyes droop half shut, obviously enjoying all the attention. Carole loosened her grip and started scratching Prancer in her favorite spot just behind her ears.

Watching the mare's gentle, contented face reminded Carole of Judy's good news a little while earlier. *It's amazing what a difference something as small as an unborn foal's tiny heartbeat can make to so many people,* she thought as she absentmindedly scratched Prancer's head. *But I guess it's that way with a lot of things. Little details can have a big impact. When Samson and I compete in the horse show a few weeks from now, we'll know that one misstep, one little penalty, could make the difference between winning and losing.*

Her thoughts wandered to her friends. A horse show was one thing, but at least there she knew what she was getting into. Real life could sometimes seem even trickier, she realized, because you weren't always sure what penalties to watch out for before they tripped you up. Her mind flashed to Ben, then to Stevie and Alex and Lisa and A.J. and Scott. They had all survived the party; Carole and her friends had made up and forgiven each other for all the mistakes and misunderstandings; Lisa and Alex were back together. But still, Carole couldn't help thinking how one night, one party, and a few little missteps had changed so many things . . . maybe forever.

ABOUT THE AUTHOR

BONNIE BRYANT is the author of more than a hundred books about horses, including The Saddle Club series, Saddle Club Super Editions, and the Pony Tails series. She has also written novels and movie novelizations under her married name, B. B. Hiller.

Ms. Bryant began writing The Saddle Club in 1986. Although she had done some riding before that, she intensified her studies then and found herself learning right along with her characters Stevie, Carole, and Lisa. She claims that they are all much better riders than she is.

Ms. Bryant was born and raised in New York City. She still lives there, in Greenwich Village, with her two sons.

You'll always remember your first love.

Love Stories

Looking for signs he's ready to fall in love?

Want the guy's point of view?

Then you should check out *Love Stories*. Romantic stories that tell it like it is—why he doesn't call, how to ask him out, when to say good-bye.

Love Stories

Available wherever books are sold.